LILY LO

AND THE

WONTON MAKER

FRANCES LEE HALL

Published by Inkshares, Inc., Oakland, California
www.inkshares.com

Edited by Regina Griffin
Cover design by May Key C. Lee
Interior design by Kevin G. Summers

ISBN: 9781947848641
e-ISBN: 9781947848658
LCCN: 2018955126

First edition

Printed in the United States of America

For Lance and Emmie

FOREWORD

In 2009, Frances Lee Hall and I founded a writing group for novelists in the San Francisco Bay Area called "Beyond the Margins." It grew quickly, and Annemarie O'Brien, Christine Dowd, Helen Pyne, Linden McNeilly, Sharry Wright, and I celebrated when Frances sold *Lily Lo and the Wonton Maker* to an international publisher. But the company closed US operations shortly thereafter and stranded Frances's dream. She passed away unexpectedly in 2016. Author Lynn Hazen, Annemarie and I—with the support of Frances's family; her agent, Marietta Zacker; and "Beyond the Margins"—were determined to bring this heartwarming story about a spunky young soccer player named Lily and her sometimes perplexing grandpa to young readers. We campaigned to raise the money to publish it posthumously, and thanks to hundreds of family members and friends who believed in Frances, you now hold it in your hands! Thank you for helping us honor the memory of a remarkable woman and writer. We hope you love *Lily Lo* as much as we do.

> —Ann Jacobus, author of *Romancing the Dark in the City of Light*

CHAPTER ONE

Who's Got Game?

WHO'S GOT GAME? SHARKS!
WHO'S GOT BITE? SHARKS!
WHO'S GOT FIGHT? OUR MIGHTY SHARKS!

Number 11, Lily Lo, waved her arms in big circles, encouraging the crowd to yell with all their might. She put her hand to her ear, signaling she couldn't hear them. The crowd responded with louder yells and super enthusiasm.

Lily squished her cleats deep into the damp grass, making a dotted footprint. That footprint made her heart race. It meant her soccer game was minutes away from starting. It meant a chance for her third-grade Leopard Sharks to show their stuff. It meant fog-filled fun!

Yes, fog!

Over the field, it rolled in, thick as bunched-up cotton balls. Most people shivered in the fog. Not Lily. The cool air filled her whole body with overflowing energy.

Parents and grandparents galore filled every row of the bleachers. Signs that read "Go Leopard Sharks" and "We ❤ Sharks" waved high above the crowd. Faces everywhere beamed with enough encouragement to fill ten stadiums.

Hurried footsteps crunched next to Lily. Rosana, Lily's pal since kindergarten, bumped her shoulder. "You ready, Lil?" she asked, her ponytail waving.

They slapped palms, held them close for a millisecond, and bumped bellies. Their red jerseys blended like one big campfire.

"Ready and more!" Lily said.

"Lily and Rosana!" Coach stood tall, her arms spread open as if holding up the world. Her gray sweatshirt was emblazoned with one word in red letters: "Sharks." "You two, get into position now!"

When Coach turned her back to gather the rest of the team, Deb, the goalkeeper, trotted up to Lily and Rosana. Her ponytail bounced high on her head, not a hair out of place. "Hey! You two." She tossed a ball in the air and juggled it quickly between her hands. "The game's starting in five minutes. Get with the team!"

Lily and Rosana looked at each other. "We heard," Lily said.

"We are," Rosana said.

Deb slapped the ball between her hands and ran to Coach's side.

"She's goalkeeper, not timekeeper," Rosana said. "She thinks she can boss us because her mom's our coach."

"Forget her, Ro," Lily said. "She's always like that before a game. Maybe she's nervous."

"Because we might go to the Big Match?" Rosana asked.

"Because we *will*," Lily said.

"Stellar!" Rosana said.

For good luck, they did their pregame ritual. Using their feet, they volleyed the ball between them three times. When they finished, they joined Anita, Julie, and Toni on the field.

With the game-starting whistle about to blow, Lily glanced at the stands.

Today was the day. She had circled it on her calendar in purple gel pen. Today Gung Gung was here to watch the game. His first time. At her game! He said he'd come, and Lily's heart had fluttered. She couldn't wait to show him her teammates, her new skills, and how practice was paying off.

At the same time, her heart stung. Sure, he was here because Mama couldn't be because of her new work schedule. And sure, he was here because someone needed to drive her. But were those the only reasons?

That was okay, she told herself. He was here now, and that was all that mattered. Right?

Lily gasped.

The seat where she had left Gung Gung was . . . empty. And the game was about to start.

She scanned the bleachers, left and right. She scanned the field, up and down.

Okay. He needed to use the bathroom, that's all. That must be it, she told herself. Or maybe he needed water. Everyone needed to use the bathroom. And everyone needed water, right? Only natural. Especially for grandpas.

And then from the pathway, emerging from the fog, came Gung Gung. His brand-new brighter-than-bright white tennis shoes acted like beacons in the fog as he casually put one foot in front of the other. His light jacket was zippered all the way up to his chin, and his cap was snug on his head. He walked to the bleachers, holding a newspaper under one arm and a blanket under the other. When he got to his seat, he wiped it, placed the blanket down—oh so carefully—and sat.

Lily exhaled. He made it.

As the whistle blew, the mighty Leopard Sharks versus the unmighty Stingray battle began.

CHAPTER TWO

Perfect Catch

THE CROWD STOMPED their feet and clapped their hands. Red-and-white pom-poms waved like wildflowers in the wind. The soccer field shook. It could've been from the cheers, or it could've been from the Leopard Sharks barreling for the ball. Either way, it was madness!

The Sharks got possession of the ball, a black-and-white blur, and passed it between them. The ball whizzed along the ground, kicking up grass. The Stingrays, in boring blue jerseys, scurried next to the Sharks in their fiery red ones.

The scoreboard showed the Leopard Sharks losing by one point. One tiny, get-it-in-there point. From all the cheers, you'd never know they were losing.

Lily huffed as she ran up the field. Pure determination pulsed through her body, and her toes buzzed. She got the ball and dribbled strong, as her knees flexed and her ankles stayed loose. The rolling ball obeyed her foot's every command.

Yes!

Lily tapped the ball with the inside of one foot, then crossed it to the other, all the way up the field.

Just as a Stingray was about to steal, she made an on-target pass to Anita, who dashed and kicked it straight to goal. The Stingray keeper missed and fell to the ground, dazed.

Goal!

Lily, Anita, and Rosana came together for a three-Shark belly bump.

The crowd cheered like it was a Super Bowl touchdown.

Lily's eyes darted to Gung Gung. *Did he see? Did he see how I assisted in that goal?*

Gung Gung no longer sat on his blanket. It was wrapped around his shoulders. He looked like he was sitting in a blizzard, not a foggy day. His newspaper was opened before him, and whatever he was reading must have been a really, really good story.

Lily's heart flinched.

"Lily Lo!" Coach called. "Focus, girl! Get ready for another pass!"

"Come on, Lil." Rosana jogged next to Lily, her breath steaming. "Gotta get moving."

"Right!" Lily said.

Rosana took off, leaving Lily behind. Down the field, Anita and Julie surrounded a group of Stingrays scurrying for the ball. They blocked them, and the crowd cheered.

Gung Gung, still reading.

One Stingray dashed out of the ocean of blue and kicked hard. The ball neared the Sharks' goal. As gasps from the bleachers filled the air, keeper Deb dived for the ball with all her might. She hugged it close as she hit the ground. Her elbows and forearms skidded along the grass.

Saved!

Gasps turned into cheers from the Shark stands.

Coach whooped like a coyote.

Gung Gung licked his thumb and turned his newspaper.

Lily got the ball and passed it to Rosana. She overshot it.

"Lil!" Rosana ran to retrieve the wayward ball, her ponytail waving like mad.

"Sorry, Ro!" Lily's hands flew to her head.

"Shrug it off, Lo!" Coach waved her hands. "Move your feet!"

Rosana got the ball and dribbled up the field to where Anita and Julie were poised and ready. Lily followed, but almost tripped.

"Focus, Sharks!" Coach yelled. "Up the field, ladies!"

As Anita, Julie, and Toni ran up the field, Lily pursued them. Her shin guards slipped, and she tugged on one as she ran. Close to the Stingrays' goal line, she hovered. Her eyes darted back and forth between the cheering crowd and Gung Gung.

Rosana's grandparents, Mr. And Mrs. Morales, although huddled close to keep warm, were up on their feet, focused on the game. They watched Rosana's every move, and hollered when she came close to the ball. Anita's grandfather had bundled himself in a jacket so cushiony, he looked like an overstuffed burrito. An overstuffed burrito that waved a wiggly "Number 1" foam finger. That thing looked alive!

Everyone cheered and watched the game.

Except for one.

Gung Gung began to turn another page, and Lily hoped, while the newspaper was shut for a split second, that he might stand up and look. Or cheer, even.

Nope.

The newspaper turned to the next page, the tip of his cap peeking above it.

In disbelief, Lily opened her arms. "What??"

"Trap, Lil! Trap!" Rosana shouted from the other end of the soccer field.

In a split second, a black-and-white haze barreled toward Lily. With her arms still opened, a blinding force stung her chest. The haze had turned into a soccer ball and landed smack in her arms.

A perfect catch.

For a goalkeeper.

Problem was, Lily was playing midfielder.

The referee's whistle blew like a teakettle. Foul, hand ball!

Groans rose from her teammates. Cheers bubbled up from the Stingray side. And then, among all that noise and clatter, Gung Gung finally looked up.

When she had fouled!

Lily looked at where she was positioned on the field. That ball might've headed straight in the Stingrays' goal, if she hadn't been in the way. Or she could've kicked it in, if she hadn't used her hands. That goal could've won the game.

Ugh.

Mr. Morales's big bear voice boomed across the field. "That's okay, that's alright, come on Sharks, fight, fight, fight!"

Rosana gave him the thumbs-up, ready to go again.

Gung Gung tilted his head to one side, as if to say *Oh well.*

Lily felt Coach's eyes upon her, but she couldn't look at her. Lily gave up the ball and stood there empty-handed.

CHAPTER THREE

Bingo

ONE BY ONE down the line, Lily and her teammates slapped hands with the winning team. "Congratulations," they said. "Good game."

Coach patted Deb's head and gently pulled on her ponytail. She called her team over for a pep talk. "Team, I've got good news and bad news."

"Bad news first," Deb said, her uniform covered in mud.

"Okay, the bad news is we lost today," Coach said.

Every Leopard Shark, except for Rosana, threw looks at Lily. Lily couldn't meet their eyes.

"Maybe we could've won if *someone* actually knew the rules of soccer." Deb put her hands on her hips, and one elbow stuck out like a torpedo toward Lily.

"Deb, please," Coach said.

"But, Mom—" Deb said.

Coach shook her head, and Deb kept quiet.

"It was a loss, but we're a team. We win together, *and . . . ,*" Coach said.

"We lose together," the Sharks chimed.

Coach leaned in, like she needed to spill a big secret. "Each and every one of you is important to this team. Each of you has a job to do. Even one Shark down, and it's total chaos! Can we let that happen?"

"No!" the Sharks yelled.

"Despite it all, this game was close. That's progress, my dears."

The Leopard Sharks high-fived one another. Rosana turned to slap Lily's palm, and Lily gave a half-hearted tap.

"And the good news?" Rosana asked.

"The good news is that we made it to the Big Match! Our fall season just flew by, didn't it? By a miracle of wins, losses, and simple arithmetic, we're in! That's awesome. Good job, Sharks!" Coach extended one hand before her.

In a circle, the Leopard Sharks extended their hands to meet Coach's. "Sharks, Sharks, Sharks! Chomp! Chomp! Chomp!" Together, their voices grew determined as their arms swung up above their heads.

The Big Match was big! Really big!

"One practice game next week—"

"You mean a scrimmage," Deb said.

"Yes, my dear daughter, thank you. A scrimmage next week, and possibly another practice after that. We'll see how our scrimmage goes. Eat healthy food, stay hydrated. Get going!"

Coach tapped Lily's shoulder. "A word, Lily."

Deb interrupted. "We need to go, Mom. We're supposed to go shopping after the game, remember?"

"Give me a sec, Deb. Go pack up your stuff." Coach squeezed Deb's shoulders, turned her toward the bleachers, and patted her backside.

Deb turned, so her mom couldn't see, and frowned at Lily.

Lily's face grew hot, and her cleats felt glued to the mud.

As the other Sharks ran for the bleachers, Rosana glanced at Lily, giving her a worried look. Lily nodded to say that she'd catch up.

"So, Miss Lily, what game were we playing?" Coach tugged on Lily's ponytail.

"Soccer, Coach."

"Ah, thank goodness! 'Cause you know, I thought maybe basketball, maybe Skee-Ball, perhaps chess . . ." Coach winked.

"Coach!" Lily knew Coach was teasing her, but she also sensed Coach was being serious. Coach did stuff like that, softened her way into things that might be hard to hear.

"And what game were you playing?"

Lily hesitated. "Catch?"

"Bingo!"

"I wasn't playing bingo," Lily said.

Coach stopped in her tracks. "Silly girl. I mean, yes, catch! Unless you want to be keeper?"

"No, I'm good." Lily moved her hands behind her back.

"Keep your head in the game, please. Not in the bleachers, or in Siberia like you were today."

"I will, Coach," Lily said, wondering what Siberia was.

"It's not like you to be distracted." Coach put her arm around Lily's shoulders. "You okay, Miss Lily?"

"Everything's fine." Lily gently shrugged off Coach's arm. "Sorry about today. I'll do better. Promise."

"Today's done. Over. Finito. Go with the flow, Lo," Coach said. "And it was a good catch . . . for a keeper," she whispered in Lily's ear. "Don't tell Deb."

Now that deserved a smile, which Lily did, big and wide.

"I'll be ready for the Big Match," she said. "I've got new shin guards."

"We're going to cream our opponent, yes we are!" Coach stopped and held up her finger. "I mean, we're going to have a fun, fair, unforgettable postseason. There's nothing like being in a Big Match."

"What do you mean?" Lily asked.

"I mean you need to experience it to see how special it is. The vibe, the rumble . . . it's big. It's the Big Match! Let's give it our best, let's stay in the game, okay? Focus, Lily Lo!"

"Got it!" Lily straightened her shoulders.

"And don't forget to tell your family, friends, cousins, neighbors, classmates, dentist—"

"My dentist?" Lily asked.

Coach bit her whistle, then took it out. "Well, maybe not your dentist, unless of course, you're related to your dentist. Everyone who can cheer us on, tell them to come. We need all the cheers we can get, Lo."

No kidding.

"Tell them to come. Or else."

"Or else what?" Lily asked.

"Or else . . . I'll call them up and sing the national anthem on their voicemail. Twice. And that will be painful. Very painful, indeed. Your mom will come, right?"

Over near the bleachers, the space next to Gung Gung looked like the emptiest, loneliest spot on earth. "My mom has a new schedule at work. She might not make it."

"Oh, I see. No worries, Lily." Coach squeezed Lily's shoulders. "We've got plenty of supporters, some quite wild and crazy, I might add."

Well, some.

"And they're all cheering for our team, right?"

Lily didn't answer.

Gung Gung sat waiting for her, quiet as can be, and folded up his newspaper.

As Lily approached the bleachers, Mr. Morales was helping Rosana with her coat, while Mrs. Morales was getting Rosana's hair out of her eyes.

"You're turning out to be quite a soccer player, Rosana," Mr. Morales said. "So fast, so swift, no?"

No. Rosana missed half her shots. But her grandparents kissed Rosana so many times that Lily lost count.

Two rows above Rosana, Anita's grandfather hugged Anita with his cushiony arms, foam finger still on his hand. She disappeared in his embrace.

Rosana spotted Lily. "Didn't you hear me warn you?"

"Obviously not," Lily said.

"Your face when you caught that ball. Total shock." Rosana's eyes widened, and her face froze in an extremely poor imitation of Lily getting smacked.

Lily playfully bumped shoulders with her. "You're not in the flow, Ro!"

On cue, Rosana hip-bumped her right back.

"Your grandparents come to every game, huh?" Lily asked.

"Oh sure! Wouldn't miss it," Rosana said. "I think they're hooked."

"Hooked, huh?" Lily said. "They know a lot of cheers."

"Anything loud, they're on it," Rosana said. "Our dinners? Loud. Watching TV? Loud. Cheering at games? Super crazy loud. Abuelo said it's in his blood. Whatever that means."

"You're lucky," Lily said.

Rosana shrugged. "I wear earmuffs half the time!"

Being loud and cheery didn't seem to be in Gung Gung's blood, whatever that meant.

With her teammates leaving, the soccer field emptied out, just like Lily's heart.

CHAPTER FOUR

Sampan Restaurant

INSTEAD OF GOING straight home after the game, Gung Gung took Lily to Sampan Restaurant. The old Chinese café stood on the corner of Mariposa and Diamond Street. Its large rectangular windows faced both streets with their shades drawn halfway, making the building look sleepy. Through the glass windows, customers could be seen pouring tea for one another. The double glass doors remained ajar, as if worn out from too much swinging. Even though the sign on the door window read "Closed," Gung Gung walked right in.

"Why does it say 'Closed'?" Lily asked.

"Too busy to change it," Gung Gung said. "Snack first."

And right on cue, Lily's stomach growled. Soccer had that effect on her, win or lose. And with today's major mistake, a little snack could make a foul sting less.

All around, customers sat at tables with mismatched tablecloths and chairs, dishing out portions of chicken chow fun.

They also sat along the countertop, hunched over steaming bowls of wonton soup. Their lively conversations—in part English, part Cantonese—sounded like crickets chirping and tweeting, rising and falling with emotion. Waiters dashed from table to table, plates of chow mein up their arms, threatening to fall but somehow always staying put.

Lily, Mama, and Gung Gung had been here for Saturday lunch many times. They'd sit near the Mariposa-side window at a small round table that wobbled, and people-watch as they ate. But today Gung Gung headed for the long, scratch-laden countertop. The scratches had been made by years of heavy cream-colored dishes, ivory chopsticks, and plastic soupspoons sliding along the counter to hungry eaters.

Lily always wanted to sit there. The red vinyl stools squeaked when you sat on them, and you could swivel at a ninety-degree angle. She hopped on one stool and swiveled to face the counter. From her perch, she could see partway into the kitchen. A big flame rose up, followed by a clang from a hot wok hitting the stove. Old Chinese guys were in there scrambling between themselves like soccer players, stir-frying like mad.

One of those old Chinese guys came out. "Ah, Walt!" he called to Gung Gung.

"Bing!" Gung Gung responded.

"Haven't seen you at Asawa's," Bing said.

Asawa's? Is that another restaurant?

"Busy," Gung Gung said, and nodded toward Lily.

Lily blushed, having no clue what they were talking about.

Bing waved his hand and scrambled back to the kitchen.

"Wonton soup, Lily?" Gung Gung didn't even look at the menu. It was left untouched, propped up between the soy sauce and hot sauce containers.

"Yes, please," Lily replied. "That's my favorite."

"I know." From a teapot, Gung Gung poured hot tea into a little cup decorated with fat plums. He touched the brim lightly as steam rose between his long, wrinkled fingers.

How did he know?

"Millie, ah!" he called to the waitress. "Two bowls house special wonton! Please."

Lily jumped. His voice boomed over the conversations in the café.

With a strand of black hair falling over her forehead, Millie swooped in and out of the kitchen, but not before placing a plate of broccoli beef in front of one man, and steamed ginger chicken in front of his friend. *"Haih ah."* She didn't write Gung Gung's order down, only turned on her heels and yelled into the kitchen, "Two bowls wonton soup! House special."

"Mein?" yelled Bing.

"Mein?" Millie yelled to Gung Gung.

Gung Gung shook his head.

That was okay. Today felt like a noodleless house special wonton day.

All this yelling! They could be at a soccer game, they were so loud. A glimmer of hope rose within Lily. Gung Gung did have a loud voice after all. Maybe even louder than some of the other grandparents.

At last Millie shuffled back and set two steaming bowls of house special wonton soup, no noodles, onto the counter.

"Mh goi," Gung Gung said to her.

Plump little dumplings bobbed in the broth next to chopped-up green onions, slices of barbecue pork, and fat mushrooms. A gingery aroma made Lily's nose tickle. And like magic, fouls were forgotten and dissolved into the steam. Lily stuck her soupspoon into the broth and slurped. "Ow!"

"Careful now," Gung Gung said. "You okay?"

Lily fanned her tongue with her hand.

"Watch now." He blew on his broth. He took one sip from his soupspoon, followed by a slurp. A noisy one.

Lily followed his example and slurped a soft wonton. She rolled it in her mouth, savoring all the flavors of pork, ginger, and garlic all mashed together. As soon as she swallowed, she ate another one right away.

"Maan maan," Gung Gung said. "Why rush? Where's the fire? Good, huh?"

She nodded, her cheeks stuffed full of wonton.

"Watch this," she said. The soupspoon's handle had a groove that acted like a little trough. Holding the spoon by its round part, Lily tipped the handle and sipped the broth, using the spoon backward. "Mmm, good."

Gung Gung shook his head. "Come on. Use your spoon right."

Half laughing, Lily wiped her mouth and turned her spoon around to use it right.

Gung Gung fished for all the extra nuggets that made the house special wonton extra special. His chopstick found fat pieces of pork, mushroom, and squid. Without spilling, he savored his food with each satisfied chew. In between bites, he glanced at Lily's disappearing wonton. "When I was your size, we made our own wonton."

What? Soup broth dripped out of Lily's mouth. A piece of barbecue pork tumbled back into the bowl, splashing broth onto the counter.

"No way," she said. "Wonton comes from a restaurant. Sometimes store-bought from the frozen section."

Gung Gung grunted. He dabbed her mouth and the counter with a paper napkin.

"My mama and me," he continued. "We made it ourselves. From scratch."

"*Your* mama?"

"Mm-hmm."

Lily had never before heard anything about Gung Gung's mama. Or anything about Gung Gung when he was her size. She tried to picture him as a boy. Did he have the same bushy eyebrows that arched as he slurped his wonton? Did he have that mole near his cheek? The hair around his ears was gray, but had it been jet black when he was Lily's size?

"You're lucky. Mama doesn't do stuff like that. Most of our dinners are frozen."

His bushy eyebrow rose. "Yes, your mama busy. Stuff, hard to do. *My* mama, your great-grandmama, she worked hard too," Gung Gung said, in between sips of tea. "Mamas do that. Work hard."

Lily looked up from her bowl. "Did your mama work in an office, like my mama does?"

Gung Gung swirled his broth, as if seeing his mama somewhere in the whirlpool of leftover green onion. "Out in the fields. Dirt all around. Hot sun overhead. Picked vegetables, washed clothes, cleaned house. All with bare hands. No such thing as vacuum cleaner. Day after day. Very busy."

Lily imagined her great-grandmama, maybe a Mama look-alike, picking vegetables in a small field. She was on her knees upon the soil, picking carrots and bok choy. Not at a grocery store where carrots were packed in plastic bags, the way Mama bought them. She threw out a weed, a stone, a beetle here and there.

"And no such thing as washing machine. To clean clothes, sometimes she hit them with rocks. Rocks found by the river." Gung Gung gently pounded the countertop twice with his hand, fingers curled. "Very clean. No holes. She knew how."

Not with a stain-remover stick, like Mama did. All that sounded hard and must've taken forever.

Gung Gung rubbed the spot where he had pounded, as if getting out a stubborn stain.

Lily rubbed her own spot. The glitter in the countertop started to shine through all the scratches. A question rose in her mind, one that she didn't expect to ask. "When she was busy and all . . . did she ever miss your soccer game?"

One bushy eyebrow raised, as if no one had ever asked him such a thing. "No soccer. We didn't play."

"Oh. Did she miss other things? Like a recital or school play?"

"We didn't have those either."

"Oh." Lily didn't know what she'd expected him to say, and she wasn't sure what she'd wanted to hear. "Guess it didn't bother you, then. When she was busy." Looking for comfort, she turned to her bowl. The last wonton lay soggy in the broth.

Gung Gung was about to take another sip of tea, but instead put his cup down. As he gazed into the kitchen, the cooks tossed bean sprouts and soy sauce chicken into the air. More flames rose and fiery light reflected back from his eyes. Some kind of memory passed before that light as the flames flickered.

"At times it did bother me, but . . ." He tapped Lily's bowl with his soupspoon, and it dinged like a tiny bell. "She knew how to make me feel better. She made me wonton. Always made me wonton."

CHAPTER FIVE

The Wave

AFTER SCHOOL ONE day the next week, Lily asked Mama if she'd take her and Rosana to the Santa Flora Aquarium. They had an assignment to draw different types of fish, and they wanted to get ideas. Since Mama had a miracle day off from work, she said sure!

When they arrived at the entrance, a ceramic dolphin and her calf swam frozen next to the door. An aquarium worker who wore his SF Aquarium cap backward checked Mama, Lily, and Ro's tickets.

Lily grabbed Rosana's hand and hurried inside.

"Incoming!" Rosana said.

"Lily Pie!" Mama called. Strands of her midnight-black hair brushed the side of her face, so she tucked it behind one ear. Rose-shaped earrings dotted each of her earlobes. Her backpack, slung over one shoulder, held M&M's and Snickers for later. "The aquarium's not going anywhere. Slow down."

Lily gave Mama a thumbs-up, and when Mama gave one back, Lily's heart swelled. A trip to the aquarium with Mama and Ro meant a double treat.

"I want to draw a starfish," Rosana said. "Because, baby, I'm a star!" She fluffed her hair and threw Lily a kiss.

Lily clicked an imaginary camera in front of Ro's face. "Say cheese."

Hands on her hips, Rosana batted her eyelashes. *"Queso!"*

"What about a stingray?" Lily asked. "They look like they're flying."

"No way. Our opponents, remember?"

Lily laughed. "Oops. That would be UN-sportsmanlike of me."

"Foul!" Rosana said.

"Better look for a . . ."

They looked at each other.

"Leopard shark!" they cheered.

Arm in arm, they headed in the direction of the giant tanks while taking steps in zigzags. Their backpacks, with drawing pads and pencils inside, bounced on their shoulders.

"Try not to break the place, ladies," Mama said, following right behind.

They passed by the tide pool exhibit. Starsfish, horseshoe crabs, and sea anemones lay in shallow water, waiting to be touched.

"We'll come back, right?" Lily said.

"Certainly can't touch and draw at the same time," Ro said.

They found a bench near an exhibit and got out their drawing pads and pencils. They peered up at the massive sea life before them in a display called "The Kelp Jungle."

Inside the two-story tank, towers of yellow-green kelp swayed like waving fingers. Fish the shape of skinny rockets zigged and zagged. An eye-shaped fish sat among the kelp, as if playing hide-and-seek. Sunshine streamed from above, making the water glisten.

One rockfish floated up to the glass, right in front of Lily and Rosana. With unblinking eyes, it stared at them, like it wanted to ask a question.

Lily waved. "Hey, fishy fishy."

The fish looked confused, its mouth in the shape of a frown. It drifted away.

"He looks more like a Fernando, not 'fishy fishy.'" Rosana said.

Lily snorted. "Fernando looks grumpy. I want a happy fish."

Rosana twirled her pencil. "Since orange is my fave color, and the starfish are orange, and baby, I'm a star . . ." She sketched a star with five points and drew bumps on its body, just like the real thing.

Lily read the "Who's That Fish?" sign. "Hey, Ro. Looks like your starfish is called a bat star."

"Nice. Like Batman."

"'They have webbing between their arms, which gives them a bat-like look,'" Lily read. "One problem about this assignment."

"What?"

"The fish don't sit still."

"Fish don't sit. But my bat star does." Ro stuck out her tongue.

Lily bonked her on the head with her drawing pad.

"My movie star hair!" Rosana said.

The more they drew and watched the fish, the more they moved with the swaying kelp. Even Mama, who was nearby checking her smartphone, swayed with the kelp.

A group of seniors swayed with the kelp.

A mother with twin toddlers in a stroller swayed with the kelp.

All felt calm . . . until a giant sound of rushing water caught their attention.

"What's that?" Lily said.

They turned the corner and another huge tank appeared. Inside it towered a massive rock that poked above the waterline. Tiny silver fish darted in and out of the rock's small holes.

As they got closer, a crashing noise made them jump.

Whoosh!

Strong waves crashed from above, sending foam, bubbles, and gushing water everywhere. All the fish scattered. The sea plants bent from the force. Soon all was calm again, and the sea plants righted themselves as the fish floated back.

"That's one force of nature," Mama said.

"Stellar!" Rosana cried.

"If we were in there, we'd be crushed," Lily said. "Cool."

"Poor fishies and Fernandos." Rosana stepped up to the glass. "They're getting canned."

"Canned?"

"Like sardines!" Rosana stood straight and still like, you guessed it, a sardine in a can.

"They look like they're on a roller coaster," Lily said.

Another wave crashed and foam filled the entire tank. Then, just as quick, all was calm again.

"Such a wavy wave," Ro said.

And then it hit Lily like a soccer ball. "You know," she said, "I can teach Gung Gung how to cheer. He doesn't know how, that's all. I can teach him."

"What? It's easy!" Rosana pumped the air with her arms. "Sharks! Sharks! Sharks!"

"I can teach him . . ."

Another crazy gush of water tumbled over the rocks.

Whoosh!

". . . the wave!"

Rosana looked at Lily like she thought Lily was crazy, which she probably did. Slowly, her eyes brightened. "Stellar!"

"Gung Gung doing the wave?" Mama said. "Well, that'd be . . . *interesting.*"

"You don't have to be loud. All you have to do is stand up and wave your arms at the right time, right?" Lily said.

"Right-oh. You need co-OR-dination." Rosana savored the "or" part.

"That'll bring us tons of luck," Lily said. "And co-OR-dination."

"Let's try it."

Lily and Rosana squatted down side by side, shoulder to shoulder, in front of the tank.

"Ready?"

"Yep!"

The seniors watched them, quite amused.

"Hold on." Mama pointed her phone at the wavers and started recording. "Action, ladies!"

Rosana rose and waved her arms. A second later, Lily threw her arms skyward as wide as scattered clouds. They bobbed up and down, first Rosana, then Lily. Their laughter grew with each little wave, giving them momentum to keep going. Their hips and shoulders swayed, creating a groove all their own. When the wave crashed again, they held their noses, snorting and giggling, and let all the good luck wash over them.

CHAPTER SIX

Still There

THE SOFA IN Gung Gung's living room was as old as, well, Gung Gung.

Lily sank deep into the cushion, its coils squeaking like mice. She didn't know if she could ever get up—the padding was as squishy as bubble tea boba.

Across the room, two cherrywood dragon statues stared at her with pearl eyes. Chinese newspapers were sprawled across a small marble table. An old ottoman the color of tangerines stood in one corner next to its matching chair. The chair's middle dipped low to match the sofa.

Gung Gung busied himself in the kitchen as sounds of running water filled his one-bedroom apartment.

Maybe after homework was done, she could teach Gung Gung the wave. They could practice in the living room. Space was a little tight, but it'd be okay. She sat up on the sofa. *Squeak.* She imagined the Sharks winning the point, and Rosana by her side. She jumped up, waved her arms high, and sat back down. *Squeak.* Up, wave, down! *Squeak.* Up, wave, down!

Squeak!

She took the squeaks as a good sign.

"Lily," Gung Gung called from the kitchen. "No jump on sofa. Get ready for homework."

"Be right there," Lily said.

She headed for the bathroom. In the hallway, three Chinese scrolls hung on the wall. Dangling by string, the scrolls were made of fabric held between two round sticks, one on the top and one on the bottom. Chinese characters painted with brush-strokes in black ink were arranged front and center. The brush-strokes varied in thickness, like the calligrapher had lightly touched the surface for some and pressed down hard for others.

Lily paused.

Even though she couldn't read the characters, she couldn't help but notice how pretty they were. How dancer-like they felt, even though they were still. All put up on the wall like that.

Chinese school started soon. Maybe she could learn to write characters like these. Goose bumps inched up her arm. Learning to speak Cantonese made Lily pretty nervous. She didn't know what to expect—and worse, Chinese school was on Saturdays.

As she passed by Gung Gung's bedroom, she peeked around the open door, hoping to see inside. She knew she shouldn't enter, but she couldn't help looking for . . .

And there it was. The picture in the copper-toned frame on Gung Gung's dresser. She and Mama had given Gung Gung the frame last Christmas. Before, he had kept the picture propped up next to his lamp. The photo's edges were getting soft, and its color was fading. When Lily suggested they get a frame for it, Mama had hugged her.

In the picture, a family of three sat at a table in a Chinese restaurant. It was Mama, Lily's dad, and Lily at six months old, dressed in lavender colors. Mama looked pretty with an orchid pinned to her blouse. Lily's dad wore a suit with a lavender tie to match Lily's dress. In the middle of the table sat a towering mound of golden fried wonton on a platter. It looked good! And grasped tight in Lily's baby hand was one crispy fried wonton. She held it as if she wanted to keep it for as long as she could.

Her dad cradled Lily on his lap like he didn't want to let her go. Except he did let go. When he died two years later. She wished she could remember him.

Lily exhaled. She only wanted to make sure the picture was still there.

CHAPTER SEVEN

Good Deal

GUNG GUNG'S SMALL round dining table was cluttered with supermarket and drugstore ads. The ads showed deals in bright, spirited colors and letters. The best cuts of meat, sparkling drinks, Golden Delicious apples—you name it, it was there on Gung Gung's table. He must have kept every ad that the postal worker delivered.

Gung Gung swished boiling water inside a teapot to warm it. From a tin container, he took a handful of oolong and threw it into the pot. While the tea steeped, he got out two teacups.

"How do you know how much to put in?" Lily asked. Mama used measuring spoons, and Gung Gung used his hands.

He tilted his head. "Just know. Want some?"

"No, thanks. I'm good."

He lifted his teacup and sipped as if tea was the most precious thing. An earthy fragrance drifted between them. "Ah, good. Hot, but not too hot. Good for your lungs. Better for your stomach."

"Sometimes it's bitter," Lily said. "That kind of tea."

Gung Gung looked at her. "Bitter okay. Sometimes bitter is good for you. Make you strong."

Lily didn't know what to say. How can something bitter make you strong?

Gung Gung read her thoughts. "Don't worry. Someday, you see. You just know."

Lily started to move one pile of ads to the floor to make room for her books. Her elbow knocked another pile, which made newspapers fall to the floor.

"Oops!"

"Careful now. Hold on." Gung Gung bent down to pick up the fallen papers. "Haven't looked at those."

"These are from last week." She shuffled the ads back together. "Want me to throw these away?"

"Not yet," he said.

While Lily set up her books, Gung Gung set down a red Sharpie. He put the ads for food stores on his right, drugstores on his left, and himself in the middle. It looked quite organized. First, he took the food ads and thumbed through each page, making "humpff" and "hmm" sounds. He read one ad for a long time, barely breathing.

"Oh, good deal. Need that," he said. "That cheap, huh?"

Lily looked up from her book and was about to answer. But really, he wasn't talking to her. His attention stayed focused on the sales.

"Yeah, okay price. Ah, better here." With the Sharpie, he made a big circle around an ad for ground pork. Other items he checked off, the Sharpie squeaking against the newspaper. Lily couldn't tell which was more important, the circled ads or the checked-off ones.

When that was done, he took out scissors connected to a red pocketknife.

"Those are cool scissors, Gung Gung," Lily said.

"Hmmm," he replied. He cut out coupons and placed them—you guessed it—in another pile. He even cut out pictures of items, that weren't coupons.

"Gung Gung?"

"Hmmm?"

"Why don't you use a smartphone? Mama gets deals on her phone. She uses an app. You could do that."

His forehead wrinkled, his head tilted. "Don't have one." He placed another coupon on the pile. "What you say? At?"

"App. I could show you how to download," Lily said. "It's easy."

He shook his head and continued cutting.

"Why do you need so many coupons anyway?" Lily asked.

"Good to save."

"Do those coupons really help?"

"Helps. Every little bit helps."

Lily looked around Gung Gung's apartment. He lived by himself.

"Why do you need to buy so much?"

Gung Gung was quiet for a moment. "Never know when you need to make something. Maybe for friends or relatives. Always need to eat."

"Like for a party?"

"Mm-hmm. Maybe for someone you don't know. Maybe for someone you don't like."

"For someone you don't like?" Lily asked. "That seems hard."

"*Especially* for someone you don't like."

Lily couldn't believe anyone would do that.

CHAPTER EIGHT

Saturday School

YEW WONG CHINESE School didn't have its own building. It borrowed classrooms from Westfield High School, a good twenty minutes from Lily's school, Seaside Shores Elementary. So when Lily and Gung Gung pulled up to the curb, handwritten signs were taped to the glass doors, announcing they were at the right place.

Gung Gung told Lily he would pick her up in two hours sharp near the front stairs. Lily's legs started shaking. She wanted to tell Gung Gung that she felt sick. That she wouldn't know anyone in class. That she couldn't speak any Cantonese! Maybe he'd notice that she felt sick and they'd go home.

Gung Gung looked at her. "Well? What are you waiting for? A bus?"

A bus?

"Do I have to, Gung Gung?"

"You have to."

"Why? Why do I have to go to Chinese school? On a Saturday?"

He grunted. "I'm Chinese. You're Chinese. We speak Chinese. Lock the door."

Lily slumped out of the car. Before she turned away, Gung Gung rolled down the window. "Have fun," he said.

She sighed. Only a grandpa would think Chinese school would be fun.

As she walked through Westfield High, her footsteps echoed in the empty hallways. Her backpack, filled with a few pencils, pens, and a frozen yogurt stick, hung heavy on her shoulders.

And there it was—room 888, with another handwritten sign on the door: "Beginning Cantonese. Levels 1–3. Welcome!" Being in level 1 felt like being in first grade again, even though she was in third grade. Would she be stuck with the little kiddies?

Lily peeked inside the classroom. Students took their seats, some switching places a bunch of times. Two boys giggled like monkeys. Their name tags read "Seymour" and "Art." They opened and closed their desks, making the hinges squeak. Clearly, first graders.

Two girls, one with round glasses, the other with oval glasses, whispered in each other's ears. Their name tags read "Leslie" and "Liz." And one quiet boy, named Toby, wrote in his notebook. Lily counted eight kids who all looked Asian, with one or two who might be half-Asian. Most of them looked close to Lily's age after all.

An entire class full of only Asian kids was something she had never seen before. Her class at Seaside was a mixed bunch of hair colors, face colors, freckles, and big smiles.

This class was all Asian. It was kind of cool.

In a billowing orange dress belted at her waist, a woman wrote on the whiteboard. Her marker squeaked with each fast, short stroke. Her shiny dark hair flowed down her back and was gathered at the top of her head with a jeweled clip. She smiled at Lily.

"Jo san," she said. She looked a lot younger than Lily expected, like an older cousin you'd play Go Fish with.

"I'm Lily."

"I'm Miss Lu. Pleasure to meet you." She extended her hand. *"Jo san*, Lily."

Lily shook Miss Lu's hand, which was soft but firm, ready to tackle Cantonese lessons.

"Jo san," said a different voice. A very familiar voice. One Lily usually heard on the soccer field and not in Chinese school.

Deb. The goalkeeper.

Deb stood next to Lily, not looking at her. She smiled at Miss Lu like she and Miss Lu were BFFs, and she bowed her head slightly.

Miss Lu shook Deb's hand. *"Jo san. Neih ho ma?"*

"Ho," Deb said. *"Neih le?"*

"Gei ho," Miss Lu said.

What did they say? Some of their words Lily knew—like *ho* meant "good" or "well." It seemed everyone except for Lily felt fine on the first day of Chinese school.

Deb stood up taller. She could speak Chinese fine, so why was she in beginning Cantonese?

"Hey, Chan," Lily said.

"Hey, Lo," Deb said. "Didn't know you were coming to Chinese school."

"You neither," Lily said. "You know Cantonese. Why are you in level 1?"

"That's just saying hello and stuff. *Everyone* knows that. Don't you speak it at home?"

"Sure, we do," Lily lied.

Deb looked hard at her. "Then why are you in level 1?"

"Because. I am."

"Where's your sidekick?" Deb said. "Rosana?"

"What? Rosana's not here."

"Never mind," Deb huffed.

"You two know each other!" Miss Lu said. "Great! You two can help each other. Always nice to have a friend in class. Makes it more fun."

There was that word again: *fun*.

Lily and Deb eyed each other, neither one saying a word.

CHAPTER NINE

Shark Hat

LILY, MAMA, AND Gung Gung could hear the music coming from Rosana's grandma's sixtieth birthday party as they pulled into the parking lot. Songs with spirited guitar strumming had turned the get-together at Sunset Park into a big neighborhood gathering. When they got out of the car, Lily didn't need the picnic area map—the music and laughter acted like a compass, pointing right to the celebration.

Streamers hung from the trees, balloon bouquets waved from the tables, and the line for the buffet stretched long. At least twenty picnic tables were filled with Rosana's relatives and friends. They ate from paper plates piled high with colorful food. Rosana had said there'd be lots of food, and she meant it!

Gung Gung stopped when he saw all the people. In his hands, he held a pink bakery box tied up with red string. "Need to check on something," he said. "After we eat. Won't be long."

"You're leaving?" Lily felt that familiar heart sting. "We just got here. And we've got lots to do."

Gung Gung looked over his shoulder toward the parking lot.

"Let's first enjoy ourselves, alright, you two?" Mama said. She held a bouquet of flowers for Mrs. Morales.

Rosana was the first to spot them. "Come on, Lil!" she cried. "My grandparents are over here."

They approached a table where a gathering of cousins, who all looked like Rosana at different ages, were planting kisses on the grand birthday queen, Mrs. Morales. A crown of white and red carnations sat upon her head, and a sparkling star ruby hung from her necklace. Her admirers tried to outdo one another for the biggest kiss and the best reaction. Then, with extra loud smooching, Mrs. Morales kissed each grandkid and patted him or her on their behind.

Mr. Morales walked toward them, a big smile on his face. And something else—something fuzzy on his head. There was a point at the top of it that looked like a fin, two felt eyes, and another point below the eyes that could be a mouth. A mouth with triangle-shaped teeth. The whole thing sat over a knitted cap with gray pom-poms tied under Mr. Morales's chin.

A shark hat.

"Like Abuelo's new hat?" Rosana said.

"Cool!" Lily said. "Where'd he get it?"

"The World Wide Web," Mr. Morales said. "For the Big Match, of course. For our Leopard Sharks!"

"Abuelo, it's called 'the web' for short," Rosana said.

Rosana's little cousins gathered around Mr. Morales like he was a superhero. He patted each head one by one and pretended to devour them. "Chomp, chomp," he growled. "Beware! I am the mighty shark!" This set off a chain reaction of squealing, bumping, running away, and then running back so the kids could be chomped again. It was hard to tell who was having more fun.

Dumbfounded, Gung Gung stood watching this man. He held the bakery box close.

"It's not a leopard shark," Rosana said.

"Who cares?" Lily said. "It's awesome!" Maybe awesome for a grandpa who didn't know any cheers. If she got Gung Gung a hat like that, at least he'd *look* like he was cheering. That was a start, to look the part. Gung Gung simply needed the right equipment, like she needed the right shin guards and cleats. The shark hat wasn't too far off from the brown cap he always wore. Well, maybe a little.

"That hat will scare our opponents outta the field," Lily said.

"He'll be the super-loudest fan," Rosana said.

"He's already loud," Lily pointed out.

"See, it works! Earmuffs!"

"My sweet, what do you think? I've got one for you, too," Mr. Morales said to Mrs. Morales.

Mrs. Morales shooed him and his cap away. "Don't ruin my hair!"

"Abuela takes after me." Rosana beamed.

"You are always beautiful, no matter what is on your head," Mr. Morales said. "Beauty that rises with the sun. Like a daffodil, bloomed and glorious!"

Lily and Rosana looked at each other. "Does he always say stuff like that?" Lily felt her face flush.

"Always," Rosana said. "Especially on Abuela's birthday."

"Ah, it's sweet. They have a lovely relationship," Mama said.

Gung Gung waited patiently to present the pink box to the shark superhero and his daffodil-bloomed wife.

At last, the little cousins scattered, and Gung Gung came forward. "Some treats," he said. "Many thanks for having us."

When he opened the box, Mr. Morales beamed. "Ah!"

Inside, little round shrimp and pork dumplings sat between layers of wax paper. Next to them sat pyramid-shaped bundles wrapped in bamboo leaves, tied with string.

"You like?" Gung Gung asked. "Har gow and pork sui mai. And joong." He pointed to the wrapped bundles. "Golden Lotus Bakery, very good."

"Joong are also known as Chinese tamales," Mama said.

"We love dim sum, right, Rosana?" Mr. Morales said.

Rosana reached for the ha gow, her fingers acting like chopsticks.

"Ay, girl, where are your manners?" Mr. Morales presented the box to Mrs. Morales.

As Mrs. Morales's eyes twinkled, she threw her arms open for Lily. "Come here, *amorcito*! *Gracias!*"

Lily disappeared within Mrs. Morales's embrace. Her bright, flowery blouse smelled like paprika and sweet carnations.

Mama arranged the flowers on a picnic table.

"Eat, eat!" Mrs. Morales said. "No one goes hungry on my birthday."

"For sixty years, we haven't gone hungry," Mr. Morales said. "For sixty years, our world has been complete with you . . . as our daughter, our cousin, our mother!"

"And?" Mrs. Morales asked, eyeing him hard.

"My cook!" Mr. Morales winked at Lily and Rosana.

Mrs. Morales's crown of carnations almost tumbled off her head as she stood to hit Mr. Morales upside his head.

The music was turned up and showered the picnic with a lively salsa beat. Rosana's parents put down their barbecue tongs at last and started dancing on the grass.

Lily caught Gung Gung spying a near-empty table far from the speakers. And the dancing. Maybe one where he could slip away, "to check something," unnoticed.

Just where did he need to go?

CHAPTER TEN

Duct Tape

BACK AT HOME, Lily threw open her closet door. She grabbed the blue bin marked "Don't Throw Away, or Else!!" and dragged it to the middle of her room.

Much to Mama's dismay, Lily liked to keep all kinds of things. "I may need it later," she always told Mama. "For a rainy day." Hence, her bright-blue costume bin was full of discarded blouses, faded scarves, and unloved jewelry. Lily kept it all. And now that rainy day was here, despite the cloudless weather outside.

When she opened the lid, Halloween appeared in the middle of her room. She marveled at the beaded necklaces, and the peacock feathers that tickled her chin.

She pulled out more things. A crown with missing rubies peeked from under a princess costume. "Too girly," she said.

A torn black cape billowed when she unfolded it. "Too vampirey."

A knit scarf full of holes was bunched into a ball. "Too fuzzy."

Soon the bin stuff was sprawled across her floor, leaving barely any room to walk let alone volley a soccer ball.

At the bottom of the bin, one hat seemed to be waiting for her.

"Oh!" she said.

When she fluffed the hat, it sprang back to life. It was a fuzzy top hat much like the one from *The Cat in the Hat*. Just like in the book, it had white and red stripes that wound around the tall section, and a white brim to shade the sun.

When she put it on, the hat grew from her head like a beanstalk and leaned slightly to the side. The fuzzy brim tickled her forehead. The red stripes matched her jersey, as if the hat knew it was Big Match time.

"This might work," she said.

Yet something didn't feel right. She didn't want Gung Gung to be the Cat in the Hat. People might get confused—or worse, laugh at him. This wasn't Halloween. This was serious! He needed to be fierce, shark-style!

She searched her room and found her stuffed animal shark.

What if she duct-taped her shark to the hat? Okay, it wasn't a *leopard* shark, but it was a *shark* shark. She remembered a TV show that proved duct tape could fix anything, even cars and boats. And she needed to fix this hat.

In the kitchen, Lily searched the drawer next to the sink. She fished out spatulas, big forks, slotted spoons, and a bent whisk. At last, her fingers touched a round, smooth object, silver in color. A fat roll of duct tape! She slipped the roll down her arm, grabbed a pair of scissors, and headed back to her room.

She positioned the shark on the brim. Not bad, not bad at all!

As she pulled off a long piece of duct tape, it crackled like popping firecrackers. The tape was extra, extra sticky. Good, that'd help in case of fog.

She looped a piece of tape into a circle, like the kind made for a Christmas garland paper chain. She stuck it on her arm, and soon sticky loops dotted her arm from wrist to elbow. That should be plenty.

When she taped the shark onto the hat, the little guy fell over.

No worries!

She used more tape and tucked it in ever so carefully, so you couldn't see it at all.

She put on the shark hat, and presto! A hat that cheered without even trying! The shark bared his felt teeth, Big Match–style. You could see this thing from miles away.

Gung Gung would be crazy excited to wear it.

CHAPTER ELEVEN

Hmmm

LILY AND GUNG Gung arrived at the scrimmage a good half hour before warm-up. A cool breeze filled with the scent of pine needles blew over the soccer field. Today they were playing the Jellyfish, whose orange-and-gold jerseys reminded Lily of Lunar New Year. Despite their festive colors, she felt ready to cream them good! Oh . . . or as Coach liked to say, play a fair, good game. Shark-style.

No one was on the field except for Deb, who was blocking balls with Coach. That lucky Deb, always having her mom at soccer. Coach punted the ball to her, then shouted how much farther and higher she should reach. Deb got red in the face but didn't stop for water. Lily hoped she had enough energy for the scrimmage.

Wearing his brighter-than-bright white fitness shoes, Gung Gung carried a stack of newspapers and a cushion under his arm. He was taking his time as usual, so Lily held on to his elbow and pulled him along. "Where's the fire?" he asked.

Huh? There was no fire.

"Maan maan," Gung Gung said. He wanted to slow down, take his time, but unlike when they were eating wontons, there was no time!

Lily was determined to teach him the wave in the minutes before warm-up. She led him to the very first bleacher row, right smack in the middle. "This is a good spot," she said.

Gung Gung hesitated before putting his cushion down on the bench. "Okay, then." He put his newspaper down next to him. "Go play," he said, waving his hand at her.

"There's something I want to teach you," Lily said.

Gung Gung was about to unfold his newspaper. "Oh?"

"The wave." Lily sat next to him. "It's a cheer where everyone in the bleachers stands up, one after the other, and waves their arms. They do it after we score a point." To demonstrate, she jumped up, waved her arms in a huge semicircle, and sat back down. "If you time it right, it looks like an ocean wave. Get it, *wave?*"

Gung Gung just looked at her.

"It takes co-OR-dination, as Rosana says."

Still, no word.

"And it keeps going until you run out of people. Then it comes back your way and you do it again."

"Hmmm."

Lily wasn't sure if that was a good "hmmm" or a bad one.

"Stand up and wave right after I stand up and wave. Ready?"

Gung Gung remained sitting, his hand on his newspaper.

"Go!" Stretching her arms as wide as she could, Lily stood and waved, imagining the fun she had with Rosana at the aquarium. The pine needle scent filled her lungs. "Whoo!"

Still as could be, Gung Gung remained sitting, confusion in his eyes.

"Keep going, wave," Lily coaxed. "Here." She jumped to his other side. "You go first, then I'll go." She waited, her legs ready to spring up.

Over on the field, Deb blocked more balls from Coach, and skidded to the grass. With her parents and grandparents in tow, Rosana arrived and headed straight to warm-ups. Anita, Julie, and Toni were stretching and doing jumping jacks. The bleachers started to fill up with spectators who talked about who was going to cream whom.

Gung Gung fiddled with his newspaper. "Need to digest lunch. Go play now."

Lily sighed, not realizing that digestion could ruin a good wave.

"Lily!" Rosana called. "Warm up with us!"

She turned to Gung Gung. "Will you wear the shark hat at least?

"Hat? Shark?"

Lily pulled out the shark hat from her shopping bag. Under the cloudy skies, it appeared brighter and bolder than in her bedroom. People in the bleachers glanced at it with amused looks.

Gung Gung's eyes widened, as big as the soccer field. "Oh. For you?"

"For *you*! I made it."

The shark hat towered in all its sharky glory.

"It matches my jersey. So they know which team you're rooting for. It shades your eyes from the sun, too. Cool, huh?"

A spark of inspiration glowed, so she put on the hat.

"Who's got game?" She pointed to the shark with her right hand. "Sharks! Who's got bite?" She pointed to the shark with her left hand. "Sharks! Who's got fight?" She raised both hands up high. "Our mighty Sharks!"

Gung Gung pointed to the cap on his head. "I have cap. Brown."

The shark hat wilted in Lily's hands. She mustered all her strength. "Please, will you try, Gung Gung?"

Her voice must've done something because his raisin-brown eyes softened. Very slowly—as slow as his driving, as slow as his walking—Gung Gung removed his cap.

When Lily placed the shark hat on his head, he looked as though he was sitting on acorns and pinecones instead of his soft cushion. He didn't say a word. When he reached up to scratch his head, he scratched the shark fin instead.

"Do you like it?"

"Hmmm."

Hopefully that was a good "hmmm."

CHAPTER TWELVE

Clip, Clip

ON THE FIELD, Coach patted Lily on the back. "So nice of you to join us on time. I love the scrimmage air in the afternoon!" She breathed in deep. "These Jellyfish are toast!"

"Creamed!"

"Sautéed!" Rosana yelled.

"Flambéed!" Lily yelled.

"Huh?" Deb cried.

"Are you ready, Lily?"

"Ready, Coach!"

Coach clapped her hands and continued down the line of players.

"You found your grandpa a hat?" Rosana said, stretching her legs.

"In my costume bin," Lily lunged one leg in front of the other. "And duct-taped a shark to it."

"Stellar!" Rosana rounded her arms in wide circles.

"You don't think it's too much, do you?"

Rosana squinted in Gung Gung's direction. She looked like she wanted to say something but changed her mind. "It's very sharky."

As Lily circled her arms, her blood pumping, a cheer rose within her. She and Gung Gung were ready to play!

Someone poked her shoulder. Hard.

"What is that *thing* on your gramps's head, Lo?" Deb stood there, her cheeks bright red. "A stuffed animal? Like for little kids?"

"Don't call him gramps," Lily said, her hands on her hips.

Deb turned away. "Whatever."

"Ignore her," Rosana said.

"I will," Lily said. But ignoring her was easier said than done. Lily's cheers inside grew faint, becoming as still as Gung Gung himself. Was everyone going to laugh at him?

She took one last glance at Gung Gung. The game hadn't started yet, and he had opened his newspaper. The shark hat, still perched on his head, peeked above a grocery store ad.

Twenty minutes into the scrimmage, the score was tied. Lily dribbled up the field, Ro and Anita close behind her. She was in scoring range, and the Jellyfish knew it. Their huffing and puffing pounced all around her. One Jellyfish scrambled way too close. At the last moment, Lily swerved and escaped her opponent's sting. She kicked that blur of a ball near the Jellyfish's goal.

Whump!

The ball missed the goal! By inches! Ugh!

Lily's knees buckled. So close, it hurt.

"Keep it together, Lo!" Coach yelled.

Lily snuck another glance at Gung Gung. With his newspaper on his lap, he was getting something out of his jacket pocket.

"Focus, Lo!" Coach yelled.

Ro and Anita were now in striking distance, so Lily mustered everything she had and scrambled near them. The ball hit her foot crooked as she passed it to Ro. The pass wobbled, but somehow Ro got it and took off.

Mr. and Mrs. Morales jumped to their feet. "Go, Rosana, you can do it! Go, girl! You've got fight!"

The whole field could hear them. The pom-poms from Mr. Morales's shark cap fluttered like mad.

Rosana's eyes never left the ball, and the way she took control of it, you knew her grandparents' cheers gave her that extra zing. No Jellyfish could touch her. Her leg swung as high as her nose as she kicked the ball.

Wham!

The black-and-white blur sailed past the Jellyfish keeper—no tentacles of any kind could've caught this ball. It sailed between the rails and rammed into the net.

Score!

Before Lily had a chance to belly-bump Rosana, the crowd erupted into the wave. It started from one end, a sea of red-and-white shirts standing up and down, arms waving, voices thundering. Mr. Morales's shark cap almost flew off as he bounced up and down pogo-stick-style.

And in the middle of it all, on that first row, sat Gung Gung, shark hat perched upon his head. One hand held his opened newspaper, and his other hand held something that glinted in the partial sunlight. Something that bit into that newspaper like a shark.

Was it . . . ? Lily couldn't believe what she saw. In Gung Gung's hand was a tiny pair of scissors attached to a red pocketknife.

He cut a rectangle out of the newspaper, put it aside, and began cutting out another section. The second piece was also rectangular, and he placed it on top of the other one.

Not only was he not cheering, he was clipping coupons. At her soccer game.

What? Oh no.

Her feet slipped and her bottom fell on the grass. Jellyfish cleats pounded past her as she looked up at the stands.

When the wave got to the end of the bleachers, it reversed and rolled back to where it had started. Within that second wave, Gung Gung sat and clipped, his brighter-than-bright tennis shoes firmly on the ground. He searched the cut-up newspaper for more coupons, and, seeing something to his liking, he clipped another one. Even the stuffed shark perched upon his head appeared to be looking for coupons.

CHAPTER THIRTEEN

Not Today

THE JELLYFISH CONGRATULATED the Leopard Sharks on their win.

"Okay, team, that score today was awesome!" Coach said. "We all played our part and rallied. Good job!" She high-fived each Shark and gave Rosana an extra-firm slap. If Rosana could have, she would've floated up to the clouds to let more sunshine in.

Lily smashed her cleats into the ground. The regrets started piling up. Her ball should've scored. Her pass to Rosana should've been steady. They'd scored the winning point, thanks to Ro, and she should be happy. But something didn't feel right at all. Somehow, this was all Gung Gung's fault.

"However." Coach held up her finger. All the Sharks stood at attention. "Since we're still a little rough around the edges, we'll need one more practice before . . ." she prompted.

"The Big Match!" Lily's teammates cheered and then slapped one another's palms, but she kept her hands to herself.

"Stay hydrated. See you at the practice. No scrimmage, just drills. We'll work on our focus, too." Coach raised her eyebrow at Lily.

Lily could've used the shark hat just then. To hide under.

"We're going for bubble tea to celebrate," Rosana said. "Bunch of us are going. See you there!" She ran to the bleachers before Lily could answer. She must've been too excited about her goal.

Someone bumped Lily's shoulder. A bump that could only belong to one annoyed and annoying keeper.

"So much for your grampy's hat," Deb said.

"Leave my grandpa alone." Lily squared her shoulders toward Deb.

"You call that wobbly ball playing?" Deb said.

"Better than letting points in!" Lily shouted.

"As if you could do better!"

"Maybe I could! Your mom said I'd make a better keeper than you."

"What? You? No way." Deb's confidence appeared to shrink.

"Time out!" Coach stood between them. "If I didn't know any better, I'd say two of my best players wanted to be cut from the team. One Shark down, and it's total chaos! Don't get me started with two Sharks down."

Deb folded her arms and glared at Lily.

Lily glared back.

"Okay, troops," Coach said, pointing to the field. "Three laps around the field."

"What?" Lily cried.

"Mom!" Deb said.

"And ten push-ups," Coach said. "Go! Move! Wait, Lil."

Lily held back.

"What did I say about keeping things between us? Deb has her faults, but she's dedicated to the game. She doesn't need comments like that," Coach said.

"Sorry," Lily groaned, feeling anything but sorry.

"I know there's a focused team player in here somewhere." Coach patted Lily's head. "She's been on vacation lately. Yep, she must be in Hawaii or the Poconos."

"The what-a-whats?" Lily said.

Coach faced Lily, her hands on her shoulders. "I'd love it if she came home."

As Deb circled around the track, she watched them talking, the scowl on her face getting deeper.

After they finished their laps and push-ups, Coach dismissed them with a wave of her hand, magic-wand-like, as if hoping to turn them back into soccer players. "Go forth and stay hydrated, Big Match-style."

The bleachers were pretty much empty. Everyone must be at the bubble tea shop already.

And there was Gung Gung, sitting on his cushion. He waited with an excited look on his face. The shark hat sat next to him, abandoned. Lily wanted to walk right past him.

"Ah, Lily, we go to the store now. Good deals. Just in time."

Lily groaned. "What store? In time for what?"

"We need to shop. I see you are upset."

"Yeah, I'm upset. Everyone's gone for bubble tea. To celebrate our win."

"Not today," he said. "Coupons expire soon." He held up his coupons, proving his point.

Those stupid coupons.

In a flash, she grabbed them. And felt something rip.

The coupons tore. Gung Gung held one half and Lily the other.

In disbelief, he looked from his half-coupons to her half-coupons. "*Ai-ya!* Lily!"

His voice rang like a fire alarm. At first no one moved.

Finally, he gestured for the coupon halves in her hand.

"I want to go home," she said, handing the coupons to him. "I want Mama to come get me."

"Come now," he said, walking to the pathway. "Things are worse than I thought."

Lily dumped the shark hat, the duct tape coming undone, into her shopping bag. As they drove away, the soccer field became distant, as if swallowed by a strange dream. Talk radio filled the car with lively conversation that made as much sense as clipping coupons during a soccer game.

CHAPTER FOURTEEN

Point, Grab

GUNG GUNG DROVE to an Asian market in a tiny mall that had popped up in the middle of the neighborhood. The mall had a nail salon, two smartphone kiosks, and a manga store all squished together. Teens milled about, slurping their sweet bean drinks through fat straws. Oh, those lucky teens.

The Asian market, with monster neon Chinese characters above the front door, took up most of the mall.

Before they got out of the car, Gung Gung opened his glove compartment and reached for a Scotch tape dispenser. Mama kept things like maps and sunglasses in her glove compartment. Why would Gung Gung keep Scotch tape in his car?

With the halves of the coupons on his lap, Gung Gung taped together a coupon.

"Help me fix." He handed Lily another torn coupon and a piece of tape. Even though she had lined up the two halves, her coupon came out crooked. Maybe it was because her hands were shaking.

Before Gung Gung noticed anything crooked, they headed to the market.

The automatic glass doors swung open, and inside, shoppers and carts filled every aisle. The whole town was here! Lively Asian music blared over the speakers.

Gung Gung grabbed a basket for himself and handed one to Lily. As if the referee had just blown the whistle, he was off. His white fitness shoes squeaked against the market floor. He wove in and out of aisle after aisle. Where did he get all this energy?

As she quickened her steps, Lily kept her eyes on the back of Gung Gung's cap so she wouldn't lose him. She dodged mothers puzzled over regular or low-sodium soy sauce. Shoppers stared at the rice aisle, filled with an abundance of long grain, short grain, brown, white, and sticky rice. Lily swerved around red "Special Today Only" signs that crowded the aisles like red practice cones. The back of Gung Gung's cap kept moving.

Dried, preserved packaged goods, all labeled in Chinese and English, filled little cubbyholes on the shelves. They gave off spicy, herby, salty scents. A tightly woven ball of turnips here, a seaweed-looking mess there—Lily took in all the ingredients. Some she recognized, like long, wrinkled strips of *foo jook*. Mama always soaked them in water overnight so that by the next day, the softened soybean stalks were ready for her oxtail stew.

Gung Gung pointed to the *foo jook*, and then pointed to her basket. Lily grabbed it along with a package of preserved black beans, dark like garden mud. Gung Gung pointed and Lily retrieved. Even though she still felt grumpy, she couldn't help but get into this shopping rhythm.

Point, grab, point, grab. What would Gung Gung point to next? Two cans of water chestnuts made their way into her basket, as did cilantro and green onions.

As her basket filled, she huffed and switched arms. She dashed around a shopping cart and wished they could get one.

"Maybe we need a cart?" she said. "I can look for one."

Gung Gung grunted. "Stay close. No wandering." He checked one taped-together coupon. From the refrigerated section, he popped two square packages of something into his basket. Next he selected a pound of ground pork that bulged under plastic wrap.

On one brightly colored display, a tin of chocolate-covered cookies caught Lily's eye. The chocolate looked velvety over the pretzel-shaped cookies. Jelly candy in large see-through canisters were stacked on top of one another, with easy-to-grab handles. Cookie sticks with smiling animals invited her to take one.

"May we get cookies?" Lily asked.

"Not today," Gung Gung said.

"Some candy?" she asked. "Something sweet?"

"Not today." Gung Gung kept walking.

Use the magic word. "Please?"

The magic wasn't working. Gung Gung didn't answer. He looked more interested in the fish counter. Lily plopped her basket down on the floor. Her arm hurt.

"Keep up now," he said.

With a loud bang, a cleaver fell against a chopping block as a man prepared someone's seafood dinner. Fish scales flew up in the air and landed on the man's dirty apron. The fish smell was both fresh and stinky. Lily couldn't take her eyes off a pile of squid in a plastic bin. Their beady little eyes dared her to touch. The flesh looked like it might stick to her finger. She reached out.

"Not now," Gung Gung said.

Lily's hand jerked back. She forgot she wasn't at the aquarium tide pool. And at that moment, she sure wished she was.

Now she really wanted to go home. He was mad because of the coupons. Well, she was mad at him first!

Gung Gung asked the fish man for a pound of shrimp. They chatted a bit, their Cantonese words unfamiliar to Lily. Their conversation turned serious, and then their voices rose with enthusiasm, competing with the store music. A good five minutes they talked. Maybe ten! And having a fun time. How long was this going to take?

"See you at Asawa's?" the fish man asked.

"Been busy. But soon," Gung Gung answered.

That restaurant Asawa's must be one good place. Even the fish man went there.

The fish man weighed the shrimp and threw it into a plastic bag. When he handed it to Gung Gung, Lily held up her heavy basket. The ball of shrimp, all gooey and raw, looked like it could bounce back when you touched it. Kind of cool.

"I can hold that." She struggled to keep her basket raised.

Gung Gung took one look at her full basket and dropped the shrimp in his. It landed on top of the ground pork. "Your basket heavy. Done now."

"I can handle it," she said. "I'm strong."

"We go now," he said, turning toward the front of the store.

Feeling extra stung, she lugged the basket to the checkout counter.

After all the items were scanned, Gung Gung presented the taped-up coupons to the checker.

The checker, a teen with pointy dyed hair, looked at him sideways.

Gung Gung nodded, like all coupons came with tape down the middle.

Soon beeps from the register ticked off each dollar saved, even from the crooked coupon. And Gung Gung's eyes brightened, as if only a good deal and a saved coupon were worth cheering about.

CHAPTER FIFTEEN

A Bigger Sip

AS SOON AS they got home, Gung Gung headed straight for the kitchen with the groceries. After Lily put her bags on the counter, she refused to look at him. In the living room, she sulked and sank way down into the sofa's worn-out cushions.

Creak.

From the kitchen, the sounds of Gung Gung clanging pots, plates, and utensils rang in her ears. He must have taken off his new fitness shoes because now his slippers shuffled against the linoleum floor. Water from the tap ran, the fridge opened and closed, a can opener roared, another small appliance rumbled. Whatever he was doing in there, it captured his full attention.

Lucky kitchen.

Lily needed to kick something. Her soccer ball sat nearby, ready to be volleyed. Her legs ached for it. And they ached for home.

"Lily, ah," Gung Gung called from the kitchen. "Come eat."

She didn't move. "Not hungry."

"Food getting cold."

She sat still and stared at the cherrywood dragons.

"I want to sleep. I'm tired!" Her last two words broke Mama's rule to mind her manners. The thought of Mama made her turn so she didn't have to look at those dragons. She curled up, knees against her chest. The tighter she squeezed herself, the more the sofa creaked and moaned.

It got so quiet, the only thing Lily heard was her heart beating.

Then Gung Gung's slippers shuffled against the rug and into the living room. A clink on the marble table told her he had set something down.

She curled up tighter and kept her eyes closed.

His breathing, slow and steady, hovered over her.

She stayed impossibly still.

He shuffled back into the kitchen. The crackle from a newspaper being opened sounded softly. Another newspaper, more coupons. Lily sighed heavily, her breath warming her knees.

Right then, the scent of soy sauce and sesame oil drifted toward her. It nudged her, and she started to unwind. She sat up and faced the pearl-eyed dragons. Her gaze fell upon a steaming hot bowl on the table. The blue rice-patterned bowl gleamed against the worn-out furniture. A matching ceramic soupspoon leaned against the bowl's edge. A paper napkin was folded into a neat triangle. Steam from the bowl rose, twirled, and disappeared. With one long breath, she inhaled. "Mmmmm."

The bowl held plump, succulent wonton, nestled among strips of barbecue pork, green onion, and bok choy, surrounded by soup broth the color of sandy hillsides. Where did Gung Gung buy this wonton soup?

After she dipped her soupspoon into the broth, she blew on it. Trying not to make too much noise, she sipped with care. Wow! She took a bigger sip. It tasted like a warm-field-day breeze. She slurped a dumpling into her mouth. It was soft but not soggy. As she chewed, her mouth filled with the flavors of seasoned pork, ginger, and fresh cilantro. Her teeth crunched bits of water chestnut. And what was this? A huge piece of shrimp!

"Mmmmmm." She started to giggle. As the warm broth filled her stomach, her terrible day started to melt away. Before she knew it, before the wonton had a chance to fall apart, the bowl was empty. She swirled her soupspoon to make sure. She lifted the bowl to her lips and slurped, inhaling every last trace of sumptuous broth. Her mouth watered, egging her on for seconds.

CHAPTER SIXTEEN

Surprise

THE BLUE RICE-PATTERNED bowl looked lonely with nothing in it. Lonely, wontonless, and filled with . . . guilt.

Lily laid the soupspoon down and wiped the tray. If she cleaned up, Gung Gung might give her seconds, and maybe forget their afternoon. She wanted that part to go away like a bad cold.

As she grabbed the tray handles, her feet slipped. The bowl slid across the lacquer tray as her heart did a two-step. She leaned forward to save the dish from crashing to the floor. As the wonton flavors lingered in her mouth, her determination for one more bite grew.

With careful steps, Lily carried the tray into the kitchen.

Gung Gung sat against the countertop reading his newspaper. He lifted his eyes without saying a word. At last she placed the tray, with the bowl and soupspoon unharmed, onto the counter. She couldn't meet his gaze.

"Uhhm mmmm," Gung Gung said.

When she looked up, he was grinning. It was a crooked grin, but a grin all the same. She took a deep breath.

"May I have more wonton, Gung Gung?" she said.

Gung Gung looked at her for a moment.

"May I have more?" She pointed to the bowl. "Please?"

For the first time all day, Gung Gung smiled wide. "Ahh!" He closed his newspaper. "Come here."

He waved her over to his round table. The ads were put away. Instead, laid out in neat little rows sat the contents of Lily's and Gung Gung's shopping baskets. Ground pork on a plate. Water chestnuts out of their cans. Cilantro cleaned. Shrimp rinsed and shelled. And the small package of something that looked like a stack of paper.

Gung Gung sat down at the table. "Make it."

"Make what?"

He pointed to the ingredients. "Wonton." His response sounded so matter-of-fact, as if Lily had asked what color oranges were.

"You made the wonton?" Lily looked at the table. There were no wonton anywhere, only the things they'd bought. Then, like sunshine peeking through chiffon curtains, it dawned on her. "Oh, like your mama did? You made wonton from scratch?"

"Mm-hmm," Gung Gung said. "*Ho mh ho sihk mei ah?* You like?"

"Oh yes," she said. "It's a million times better than Sampan Restaurant."

"I know," he said. His grin turned mischievous, as if he had wanted to tell this secret for years.

"Is it hard to make?"

"Not hard. Takes practice."

Like soccer, Lily thought. "Can you show me how?"

"Mm-hmm. *Choh dai.*" He pointed to the chair.

Lily planted her bottom on the chair. It didn't swivel like at Sampan, but that was A-okay.

To her surprise, Gung Gung began to hum. Sunlight from the window streamed behind him, making the kitchen inviting. The warm weather seemed to make the memory of torn coupons go away.

"What's that?" Lily pointed to the square beige stack of something.

"You'll see," Gung Gung said.

Like at the supermarket, when he pointed, she got. He pointed to the ground pork and then to the food processor. With a wooden spoon, Lily scooped a hunk of pork into the processor, along with a few water chestnuts. Then Gung Gung tore the cilantro into small pieces and gave a handful to Lily. She slipped that into the processor too. He pointed to the soy sauce, and she shook a few drops over the meat. With the processor covered, he pointed to the "Chop" button.

When Lily pushed the button, the motor roared, and they both jumped. Then they chuckled at their fuss over a little noise. The food swished and swirled until it became a smooth paste.

"What about the shrimp?" she asked.

"You'll see." He retrieved an egg from the refrigerator and put it into Lily's hands. She cracked it open into a rice-patterned bowl that he placed in front of her. With his fork whirling, Gung Gung whisked the egg into a smooth yellow puddle.

Next, he separated a thin square piece of dough from the stack. "Wonton *pei*. Skin." The skin looked like paper but was thicker and dusted with flour.

Lily held one on her palm and sniffed it. "This is wonton?" she asked.

"You'll see. Watch, okay?"

Lily nodded.

"Yat," he counted. Onto the skin's center, he placed a mound of pork filling, no bigger than a marble. On top of that, he popped a whole shrimp. "Surprise."

The warmth in Lily's stomach grew stronger and reached down to her soccer toes.

"Yih." With his fingertip, he moistened the skin's edges with the egg batter. Then he folded the opposite corners of the wonton *pei* together to form a triangle.

"Saam." And finally, he bent the middle and sealed the two corners together. He held the wonton up like a soccer trophy.

Lily shot her hands skyward. "Score!"

"Try now." Gung Gung pointed to the *pei*.

Lily separated one piece of skin from the stack. It was easy to get two pieces stuck together. It took some careful separating, but she succeeded in taking one without tearing it. She followed along as best she could.

One, two, three.

With expert hands, Gung Gung dipped, wrapped, and twisted. His fingers danced, applying knowing pressure to the dough.

Yat, yih, saam.

With uncertain hands, Lily fumbled with the filling, making the fattest wonton ever. The shrimp poked right through the skin.

A, B, C.

Lily pressed too hard on her next wonton and it broke apart. Gung Gung leaned over and fixed it. Under his fingers, the dough repaired itself. "Keep going. Do it like you mean it."

"Rosana taught me how to count in Spanish. Want to learn how?"

"Sure," Gung Gung said as he wrapped.

"Uno, dos, tres."

"Ah!" Gung Gung copied Lily as best he could. He sounded good, speaking Spanish with his accent.

Finally, without trying too hard, without thinking too much, Lily folded the wonton into the finest one ever. It didn't bulge or lean over, or even tear. It was perfect. She held it right up. "I did it!"

Gung Gung inspected the little dumpling and smiled as wide as the ocean. *"Ho leng!"*

"Really?" Lily said. "You think it's beautiful?"

He nodded.

The way he said *"ho leng"* reached in and touched Lily with light. A light brighter and bigger than any wave could give. He didn't stand on tired feet and wave his arms in a big circle. Didn't have co-OR-dination. Didn't shout it at the top of his lungs. He didn't have to.

CHAPTER SEVENTEEN

Not-So-Good Luck

"WE WILL BOIL wonton, and when they float to the top," Gung Gung said. "They are done. We eat."

That was right. The wonton weren't cooked yet. Even so, they looked ready to pop in your mouth.

"Was that how your mama cooked them?" Lily asked.

"That was one way."

They worked until their fingers stuck together with ground pork and dough. Little by little, right before their eyes, the contents of their shopping basket disappeared. And in their place, little wonton sprang up like mushrooms in a field. Lily and Gung Gung sat back and admired their work.

"Did you and my mama ever make wonton? When she was my size?" Lily asked.

Gung Gung sat still as if trying to remember. "Ah, once upon a time we did. Not too often."

"She never made wonton with me."

"Maybe you can remind her how it's done."

"I can't remember all the steps," Lily said.

"I will write it down for you."

"She's way too busy anyway."

"Lily, you are never too busy for wonton."

Gung Gung chuckled, a sound as sweet as sticky breakfast buns. He rose from the table and put water into a stockpot. The gas stove turned on with a swoosh. "Big Match is soon, yes?"

"Oh yes! Usually I play midfield, but I may be a forward at the Big Match. Coach also says I could make a good keeper someday. A goalkeeper."

"Keeper?"

"Yes, like Deb. Coach is her mom. The keeper is the one who blocks all the balls so the other team can't score."

"Ah, yes. The one who blocks the balls. The unhappy one."

More like the awful one, Lily thought. "What do you mean?"

He shrugged, then fussed with the flame as he kept a careful eye on the water. "She does not smile like you and Rosana do. And you two argue. Bad energy."

Lily felt one knee sock droop. "She didn't like your shark hat. She called you gramps."

"Oh, I see. Hat." Gung Gung chuckled to himself. "Not good for game, you two arguing. Not-so-good luck. Makes you tired. Grumpy." He returned his gaze to the water. "Let Deb be Deb. You never know another's pain, Lily. You never know."

When the other knee sock drooped, she grabbed both socks and pulled. "I'm sorry about your coupons, Gung Gung."

Gung Gung's crooked grin came back. "We all get tired sometimes. Good thing we have wonton to build our strength up, yes? Smiles return. Now, Rosana, always smiling. She must eat wonton."

"I've never seen her!"

"I see why you two are friends."

"She's my best friend," Lily said, her knee socks staying put.

"I know. Good energy."

"We do everything together."

"I know."

"How do you know?" Lily scratched her head. During the game, Gung Gung had his eyes on his newspaper, not on her and her friends. Once, Mama had said that she had eyes on the back of her head, whenever you thought she wasn't watching you. It was as if Gung Gung had eyes that could see through his newspaper. Maybe he saw more than Lily thought.

"Just know." He started humming.

While he stood watch over the boiling water, Lily went into the living room and came back with her soccer ball.

"Can I show you something, Gung Gung? I'm not tired anymore."

"Not the wave again?"

"Something we do for good luck. We're going to need it for the Big Match. Want to see?" Standing next to the round table, she tossed the ball and caught it with her foot. Feeling confident, she tried again, this time tossing it much higher. At the same time, Gung Gung turned from the stove and gasped. The ball came down fast, and Lily couldn't control it. It slammed against her foot and flew up at a sharp angle. Lily reached out, but it came crashing down on their table.

Right on top of the wonton.

Oh no!

The plate flew into the air, somersaulted once, and little wonton tumbled and landed smack on the linoleum floor. The plate broke into three sharp pieces, splitting apart the pattern of a dragon. Lily dared not move, all her breath gone. Her beautiful wonton lay smashed on the floor.

"*Ai-ya!*" Gung Gung took Lily by the shoulder, hurried her to the side, and raced to turn off the gas stove. When he grabbed a broom from the closet, she wanted to help, wanted to make it all okay. Instead, her sneakers stuck to the floor. She couldn't bear to look at the mess.

Shaking his head, Gung Gung began to sweep. The dirty broom bristles brushed aside their newly homemade wonton.

His crooked grin vanished as the wonton disappeared into the garbage can. He spoke an unfamiliar phrase in tones that stung Lily's ears, as if he wanted her to go away. For once, she was glad she couldn't understand.

CHAPTER EIGHTEEN

Asawa's

SINCE IT WAS a half day at school, Lily waited with Rosana in the car line at twelve fifteen sharp. The line crawled inch by inch as classmates hopped into their cars. Lily looked for Mama's car but didn't see it.

"Really? It all fell on the floor?" Rosana asked.

"Really," Lily said.

"You saved nada?" Rosana asked.

"Nada. We'd just made them. Then, ka-blam! All over the floor."

"It must've been cool when all the wonton flew in the air! Dumpling shower!"

"Ro!"

"All that work!"

"He was so mad," Lily said.

Or sad, Lily couldn't tell which. Sadness would be really . . . sad. "We didn't say much after that."

"There's my *abuelo*. And hey, look who's here," Rosana said.

To their surprise, Gung Gung pulled up in his car.

As she jumped into Mr. Morales's car, Rosana mouthed the words "Good luck."

"I didn't know you were picking me up, Gung Gung," Lily said as she slipped her backpack into the back seat.

Gung Gung didn't look mad anymore. Maybe things between them were okay. Maybe he wanted to get lunch at Sampan.

"Something came up at your mama's work. Last minute."

She sank into the car seat. *Oh,* Lily thought. *He's driving me because he has to.*

"Got homework?"

"Not much. Only spelling and math," Lily said.

"Good. You can finish after," he said.

"After?"

"Need to drop by first."

"Drop by?"

"You'll see."

"Are we going to the Asian market?"

Gung Gung shook his head.

"Sampan?"

"You'll see," he said.

They arrived at Sunset Park, where Rosana's *abuela* had her birthday party. But instead of going to the park, they headed for a building near the parking lot. The sign on the front door read "The Ruth Asawa Senior Center. All are welcome!"

"This is Asawa's?" Lily raised her eyebrow. A senior center didn't sound very fun. Nobody would be her age. Was it a place where old people sat around and did nothing?

Gung Gung opened his trunk. "Here. Help me bring these."

Lily helped carry two bags of groceries while Gung Gung picked up two cardboard boxes from the trunk. The bags were filled with apples, bananas, onions, bok choy, and other vegetables.

When they entered the center, a gust of warm air and the smell of coffee greeted them.

All around them, seated in soft chairs, seniors chatted with one another or read books and magazines. One man snored softly while sitting up. One lady drew a needle through fabric attached to a hoop while her neighbor knitted what looked like a cap.

"Walter, so good to see you," the knitter said. "You've got help today."

Gung Gung nodded. "Rose, my granddaughter, Lily."

"Hi," Lily said.

Rose's perfume smelled just like her name. "So this is Lily," she said. "We hear a lot about you."

"How you play soccer," Rose's neighbor chimed in.

"And go to Chinese school."

"And your best friend is Rosana."

Lily blushed and glanced at Gung Gung.

Gung Gung stood there and shrugged.

"Ho leng," Rose said to the needlepoint lady.

"Haih ah," she agreed.

The compliment made Lily blush even more.

"We so enjoy your grandfather's cooking," the needlepoint lady said. "We look forward to it. Especially the dumplings."

"Everyone does." Rose looped yarn around her needle. "Reminds me of home."

Again, Lily eyed Gung Gung. *He cooks here?*

In one corner, a group of four men played mahjong. Their rectangular ivory tiles clacked against one another, making lots of noise.

They stopped swirling their tiles and waved. "Walt! Long time no see."

Gung Gung nodded, his arms full of boxes.

"Next game?" a man with a gray beard asked. "Save you a seat."

Gung Gung shook his head. "Short visit."

The four players groaned. "Guess he doesn't like us anymore," one man said. "Yeah, better company." He winked at Lily.

"Well, if no Walt, at least we get to eat good." The players laughed. They stacked their tiles two pieces high in neat rows ready for play.

Lily and Gung Gung passed by several rooms. Seniors circled and stretched their arms skyward. Country music played in another room. People danced the same moves all in lines.

All the activity filled the center with so much energy and a feeling Lily couldn't name. Some kind of lightness.

They reached the dining room that was scattered with round tables and chairs. A simple vase with daisies sat on each table. Quiet violin and cello music played from speakers. Many people were seated, waiting for lunch to begin. They sipped coffee or tea and nibbled on Oreos and Fig Newtons.

"Over here." Gung Gung backed into a swinging door that led to the kitchen.

Steam, garlic smells, and sounds of pots clanging overwhelmed them.

The kitchen was covered in stainless steel from head to toe, from the countertops to the refrigerators. A cook dressed in a white apron chopped up carrots and green onions. His blade worked fast against the chopping board, making a noise like popcorn popping. Another cook pan-fried noodles in a large wok, tossing them in the air like a wayward soccer ball.

And emerging from the activity was Bing, the Sampan Restaurant cook.

"Ah, Walt!" he yelled.

"Bing!" Gung Gung said.

"You're a lifesaver," Bing said. "Shorthanded today."

Gung Gung put the two boxes on the counter next to the stove, like he knew exactly where to go. "Boil water, please," he said to the cooks. "Your bags over there, Lily."

Right away the cooks unloaded Gung Gung's apples, bok choy, and onions like it was their usual routine.

A woman dressed in a warm, fuzzy sweater with a smile to match greeted them. Her glasses hung from a chain around her neck.

"Walter," she said. "Who do we have here? Must be Lily."

"Yes, my granddaughter." Gung Gung was beaming. "Lily, this is Miss Ruth."

"Oh! Is this place named after you?" Lily asked.

"Oh no, but what a compliment. Our center is named after Ruth Asawa, an artist we all admire."

"Cool," Lily said.

"Miss Ruth's the boss," Gung Gung said.

"More like the humble go-getter. Nice to meet you, Lily. Wonton day?" Ruth pointed to the boxes.

Gung Gung's eyes sparkled. From the boxes, he took out a few dozen plastic-wrapped trays. He made sure not to drop them, Lily noticed. Row upon row of wonton appeared, ready to be boiled.

"Sale on pork and shrimp, so made extra," Gung Gung said. "Took a few days. Not as fast as I used to be."

"Wonderful! It's been a while since we've had your wonton," Ruth said. "Everyone's been asking about it. Sometimes we order from Sampan." Ruth nudged Lily. "But our folks only like your grandpa's. I think it's the shrimp."

"That's the best part," Lily said.

Gung Gung waved his hands, shooing Ruth's compliment away. His ears were turning pink.

"We've really missed it. But it's okay. Lily has soccer games, right? We know you've been busy."

Gung Gung glanced at Lily, then looked away, like he didn't want her to hear that.

"I can make more again," Gung Gung said. "After Big Match."

"We can't wait," Ruth said.

A pang shot through Lily's heart. Gung Gung had been making wonton for his friends here. And maybe for people he didn't know. Or didn't like, even.

He'd had to stop. Because of her. And he'd never said anything about it.

CHAPTER NINETEEN

Big Mouth

AFTER A SNACK break, Lily and her classmates opened their Chinese writing books.

"When we write our characters, it's as if we're painting pictures," Miss Lu said.

Seymour yawned while Art twirled his pen.

Deb held her black felt-tip pen like a weapon, ready to tackle the paper.

Lily sat up straighter. She loved art and painting, like when she and Mama had painted roses on their backyard bench. In her book, each character's stroke had a number and an arrow next to it. Something like paint by numbers.

"The basic strokes you must learn and absorb into your blood," Miss Lu said.

Both Seymour and Art shivered. "Eww."

"Here's the first one." Miss Lu drew a stroke that looked like a raindrop.

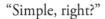

"Simple, right?"

"I can do that," Seymour said without raising his hand. "Easy peasy."

Miss Lu put one finger to her lips. She drew more strokes, her marker sweeping the whiteboard.

"Straight like a tabletop," she said.

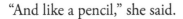

"And like a pencil," she said.

"One is the side of a mustache, the other a horse's tail," she said.

"With hooks on the end. Like a comma," she said.

"And half a box," she said.

"You try now. Draw each stroke ten times," Miss Lu said.

"Even the raindrop?" Seymour asked. "Ten times?"

"Especially the raindrop," Miss Lu said.

As Lily practiced, she discovered the strokes with little hooks were fun to make. Like adding a little hop on each end.

"Drawn together, these strokes make up the big picture, the whole character," Miss Lu said. "Drawing the strokes in order is important too. Otherwise you'll just be a copycat. Order shows discipline, clarity of purpose, and a pure heart."

Seymour raised his hand. "How can writing show your heart? You can't see my heart. You can only see my T-shirt."

Art pointed to the Spiderman graphic on his shirt. "Me too. And what's *pure* mean?"

"It means being clean," Deb said. "Unlike your hands."

Art wiped his hand on Spiderman.

"Free yourself from judgment." When Miss Lu eyed both Art and Deb, they turned back to their papers. "There are numbers in your workbook. To remind you which stroke to draw first."

A collective "Ohh" rose from Lily's classmates.

"Characters deserve your respect and attention," Miss Lu said.

Something warm ran through Lily's body. Each stroke, each character with numbers and arrows, looked like part of a map leading to someplace special.

"If you use your imagination, many characters look like their meaning," Miss Lu said. She drew a vertical stroke, followed by a horizontal line that turned a corner downward, and closed the frame with a straight line. "Ideas?"

"It looks like a box," Deb said.

"Does it mean *square*?" Liz asked.

"Or *rectangle*?" Leslie asked.

"Does it mean *empty*?" Deb asked. "There's nothing inside."

Miss Lu shook her head.

Lily imagined the boxlike character was in the shape of someone cheering. Cheering so loud that it was impossible to close. She raised her hand. "Is it *mouth*? One that's open, maybe laughing?"

"That's right," Miss Lu said. "This is the character for *mouth. Hau.* Good, Lily."

Quicker than a blink, Deb threw a look at Lily.

They all repeated *"Hau"* and wrote it in their notebooks.

"Hey, look! I drew mine super big, so now it's *big mouth*!" Seymour said.

The class erupted in laughter. Miss Lu tapped her marker on the whiteboard, but even she couldn't keep from smiling at that.

Lily turned to see if Toby got the joke. He pointed to his character *hau* where he had drawn two eyes above it. He made little dashes for lashes. Lily leaned over and drew a dot for the nose as they both tried to keep from laughing.

On the other side of Toby, Deb watched Lily and Toby laughing. She huffed when she saw Toby's version of *hau*. As she wrote *hau*, she dug deeper into her paper with each stroke.

Miss Lu held up her hand for silence. "When you add strokes, it becomes a different character." She added strokes inside *hau*.

"Any ideas?" she asked.

"It looks like a bunch of squares," Seymour said.

"A present?" Leslie asked.

"A grid?" Deb asked. "Like in our Chinese notebooks?"

Lily studied the character. A field with trees took shape in her mind. Like when her family had visited the Christmas tree farm. Fat evergreen Christmas trees spread out for miles in long rows across the hillside.

"Is it a field, like one for Christmas trees?" she asked.

Deb made an annoyed sound through her mouth. "I don't see trees at all."

Miss Lu nodded. "Very close! A field, yes, but not for trees. It means rice field. *Tien.* Nice, Lily. You are very perceptive. Repeat, class."

The class repeated *"Tien."* Except Deb, who folded her arms and glared at her paper.

"How about this last one? Characters do not always look like their meaning." She drew a horizontal line, followed by a diagonal stroke falling left to right. And finished with *hau.*

No one said anything for a while.

"A house?" Seymour said.

"An umbrella?" Leslie asked.

"A swing?" Liz asked, her glasses fogging up.

"A garage?" Deb said. "To put your car in?"

Lily imagined the first two strokes as someone's leg kicking something, like a soccer ball. But it was too square for a ball. Maybe something smaller, like a stone.

"Stone," Lily said. "Does it mean *stone*?"

Miss Lu's eyes lit up. "Yes! Good job, Lily. This is *stone. Siet.*"

"What?" Deb said. "It doesn't look like a stone."

"Characters don't always look like what they mean," Lily said to Deb.

"Whatever," Deb shot back.

"Practice writing now," Miss Lu said. "Keep silent. Focus."

Lily relaxed into the strokes for *hau*, *tien*, and *siet*, mindful of their order. Her hand and fingers controlled the pen, as it created strong lines. As whole characters formed on her paper, everything else faded.

Chinese school began to feel not so bad after all. She wondered if Gung Gung knew how to write characters.

A pen dropped and slid near her desk. It belonged to Deb.

When Deb picked it up, she looked over Lily's shoulder. "Show-off," she whispered.

"You too," Lily whispered back.

CHAPTER TWENTY

Big Match

ON THE DAY of the Big Match, a great, big miracle happened on Lily's soccer field.

Sun!

No fog as far as the eye could see, or as far as flip-flop feet and short-sleeve arms could feel. An excited crowd—no, a crazy-happy crowd, sitting sweaty and thigh to thigh—filled the bleachers.

The Leopard Sharks' spitfire red covered one half of the bleachers, while the Stingrays' boring blue covered the other. All that was needed was white and they'd be ready to celebrate the Fourth of July. Lily figured the Sharks' supporters must've heard Coach's warning and wanted their voicemail free from national anthem mayhem.

To add to his shark hat, Mr. Morales brought a cowbell. He rang it extra, extra loud.

Ring-a-ling-a-ling! Ring-a-ling-a-ling!

The scoreboard showed that the Sharks were winning 3 to 2. A few minutes left until they were crowned champs! Lily tasted victory and kicked up her heels.

Rosana got the ball and kicked it toward the Stingrays' goal. But the Stingray goalkeeper was quick and blocked it like a pro. Everyone was playing their A game today.

"Keep going, Rosana!" Mr. Morales yelled.

Ring-a-ling-a-ling! Ring-a-ling-a-ling!

Still on her toes, Lily headed for the Sharks' goal line, poised to get the ball back. She glanced up at the bleachers. The crowd was on its feet, except for one grandpa right on the top row.

Gung Gung.

Leopard Shark parents, grandparents, kid sisters, and cousins cheered with thunderous team spirit. They were so fired up and ready to celebrate their victory that someone started doing the wave. Arms and the color red flew up and down with joy.

The wave neared Gung Gung.

He watched it come closer, like he was waiting for a bus. Just as it was about to crash over him, he fiddled with his cap, as if to make sure it was on snug.

And then it happened.

Like wonton floating to the top of boiling water.

The wave arrived and Gung Gung stood up. Waved one arm. And calmly sat back down, a little late.

Wow!

Gung Gung, *her* Gung Gung, did the wave!

Goal line happiness shot through Lily.

"Whooooo!" she shouted, her arms raised high. "Hey, Gung Gung! Good job! You did it!"

Gung Gung nodded, but then a horrified look came across his face. He stood up and pointed at the field.

Quicker than a flash, the ball sailed past Lily, like she wasn't even there. It headed straight to the Sharks' goal. Deb huffed, reached up, and . . .

Missed.

Score for the Stingrays.

Leopard Shark joy turned into Leopard Shark shock.

The Stingray side erupted in cheers that made the little ones cover their ears.

The scoreboard changed: 3 to 3. Lily's teammates looked at one another, full of alarm.

Lily felt her stomach sink to her soccer toes.

"Lo!" Deb shouted, coming up from behind Lily. "That one was yours. What gives?"

"I don't . . . ," Lily said.

"You should be benched," Deb said.

"But my grandpa just did the—"

"Geez, not your gramps again."

A bee-sting-like feeling surged through Lily's body.

That was it.

Before she knew it, she turned and pushed Deb.

Hard.

Deb jerked and fell backward, right smack onto her behind. A look of shock covered her face. She rubbed her elbow where a scrape was starting to turn red. Tears filled her eyes.

"Deb!" Coach yelled.

Those tears made Lily gasp. What had she done?

"What happened, Lil?" Rosana said, running up to her. "Did Deb fall?"

"I . . ." Lily's voice shook. "Pushed her."

"What?" Rosana said. "Why? We might get a penalty! We could lose!"

"It wasn't . . ."

Rosana didn't wait for Lily to finish, she bounded away.

Lily had never seen Rosana so angry with her. She wanted to explain what had happened, but no one was giving her a chance. Shouts and groans rang out from every which way.

The referee held up a red card and pointed to number 11.

Number 11.

Lily Lo.

Lily was out of the game!

Mr. Morales put down his cowbell. The Sharks fans yelled in disbelief.

Lily's teammates turned to Lily, their faces full of accusations and disappointment they didn't know what to do with.

They were one Shark down.

Total chaos.

Lily slumped onto the bench, the hardest bench in the world. She couldn't look at Coach.

Something made her look up into the bleachers, even though she didn't want to. Among all the uproar and fuss, Gung Gung stood there, calm as tea leaves. Their eyes met for a brief moment.

The worry in his face made Lily's eyes fill with tears, and she looked away.

Unable to move.

CHAPTER TWENTY-ONE

Dear Lily

LILY STORMED INTO her bedroom, took off her cleats and shin guards, and threw them in the closet. They crashed against shoeboxes and board games, making a giant mess. Maybe she'd never take them out again.

The shark hat sat on her chair. She ripped the shark right off the striped hat, the duct tape screeching. The poor stuffed animal lay squished in her hands. Now what had she done? She sat on her bed and hugged the shark to her chest.

A knock sounded at the door. Mama peeked in. "Lily Pie."

"Not hungry."

Mama sat on the bed next to her. "I'm really sorry about the game."

Lily hugged the stuffed animal tighter.

"Gung Gung said there was a penalty."

"Because of me. And now the whole team hates me. Even Rosana."

"Rosana is your best friend."

Was.

"It's a really tough loss," Mama said. "And I know it's going to hurt for a while."

"We were ahead. We were so close."

"I know."

"Then they tied. Then they scored the winning point and . . ." Lily leaned her head against Mama's shoulders.

"It also sounds like you need to apologize to someone," Mama said.

Lily winced and felt like crawling into the closet with her cleats.

"Gung Gung left something for you." She handed over an envelope.

"For me?" Lily asked.

Mama squeezed Lily's shoulder and got up to make dinner.

Sure enough, the neat handwriting on the envelope showed it was addressed to her.

Miss Lily Lo.

The "Miss" part surprised her most.

She slipped her thumb under the flap and took out the letter. Beautiful Chinese calligraphy swept across the page. It was written with a brush dipped in midnight-black ink. Like the scrolls that hung in Gung Gung's hallway.

But these were different. The writing wasn't as fancy as on the scrolls, but more . . . Gung Gung–like. Simple, calm, neat. It showed skill that must've taken a lot of practice as a young boy. These characters looked like someone gave each stroke his respect and attention. Like he must've felt the same way she had felt when she worked on her characters—that each stroke took you to someplace special.

Another page was written in neat English with a ballpoint pen.

Dear Lily,
How to make wonton. In case you try at home.
Gung Gung

The next page revealed a list of all the ingredients from her shopping basket. Gung Gung had written down instructions in wonton-making order, each step with a number beside it. The ingredients lined themselves up on the list, ready to go.

She reread each number, each step that created something delicious. Something that she and Gung Gung had made. Together.

His words floated through her mind. *She knew how to make me feel better.*

Lily bounded into the kitchen. "Mama! We need to go shopping. I need to make wonton."

"Make wonton?" Mama said. "Now?"

"Gung Gung and I made wonton." She faced Mama. "He laughs when he makes it. He has this crooked grin."

Mama smiled, as if remembering herself. "It's a lot of work. I'm not sure how to make . . ."

Lily grabbed Gung Gung's letter, careful not to crinkle it. She waved the recipe high in the air. The characters in sweeping ink and words in ballpoint pen beamed bright and strong. "I know how."

CHAPTER TWENTY-TWO

Treasure

AFTER SHOPPING AT the Asian market, Lily and Mama sat side by side at their dining room table. The wonton ingredients lay before them in a neat row, the way Gung Gung had prepared them. Lily passed her finger down every item on the list to double-check they had everything. They were set.

"Are you sure you know how it's done?" Mama took the paste out of the food processor.

"I'm sure." Only Lily wasn't sure. She knew how to combine all the ingredients together—that was the easy part.

"Oh. We forgot to put the shrimp in the food processor," Mama said.

"Wait for it." Lily dabbed a small mound of filling onto the skin. Then she popped in a whole shrimp. "Surprise!" The shrimp lay curled around the filling.

Mama smiled. "Only Gung Gung does that. Most people grind the shrimp in with the paste." She peeled the shell off one shrimp.

"Gung Gung *and* his mama did that," Lily corrected her. "His mama did it all by hand. No food processor. Cool, huh?"

"His mama?" Mama put her shrimp down. "He told you that?"

Lily nodded. "He and my great-grandmama."

"I didn't know they made wonton." Mama leaned forward. "What else did he say?"

"When she made wonton, he liked it a lot. Made him feel better, even though she was busy doing chores and picking vegetables." Lily paused. "Busy, like when you can't go to my games."

As she patted her fingers with a napkin, Mama lowered her eyes. "Even though I can't be at your games, I'm cheering for you." She reached for Lily's flour-dusted fingers. "You know that, right?"

Lily held on to Mama's hand, sticky from the shrimp. "I know, Mama. It's okay. Gung Gung doesn't cheer at the games like you do, but it's nice he's there. He's got his own way."

Mama grinned, a crooked one much like Gung Gung's.

A question tap-tapped Lily, ready to punt. "He said he made wonton with you, once upon a time."

"Once upon a time? As in a fairy tale?"

"That's what he said. Only I want it to be real. His mama made it when he was sad. But we can make it for fun. Can we make wonton more often?" Lily asked.

Mama smiled. "Yes, Lily Pie, we can. It'll be a real treat for us both."

Together, they returned to the task at hand.

The part about folding the wonton jumbled in Lily's memory. She twisted one wonton together, but right away it fell apart. Maybe she hadn't used enough egg wash. Another one ripped, with the shrimp bulging out like a potbelly.

"Who would eat that? Gung Gung wouldn't." Lily's frustration grew as Mama tried to fix all the broken parts. They created a complete, sorry mess, almost as terrible as broken wonton on the floor.

Then the scent of sesame oil and cilantro surrounded them. An image of the best bowl of wonton soup ever grew in Lily's mind. She placed one wonton skin on her palm and held it. By itself, it looked like nothing special. Only a flat piece of dough dusted with flour.

Only Lily knew better.

When she sniffed it, Gung Gung's cheer sang in her heart.

Yat, yih, saam. Yat, yih, saam.

His accent. The tone of his words. His laugh.

Ho leng.

She could do it.

"*Yat,*" she counted. Her fingers danced around the wonton skin and filling. She took her time, finding a rhythm all her own. She started humming. Mama started humming too. And soon, the perfect dumpling appeared before her. Its little shape was simple, yet held a treasure.

Just like Gung Gung.

CHAPTER TWENTY-THREE

Good Energy

LILY BORROWED MAMA'S smartphone to call Gung Gung. "Thank you for the recipe, Gung Gung. *Dor dje.* Your Chinese writing is really pretty."

"Glad you like it," Gung Gung said.

"We're learning our strokes in Chinese school. Maybe I can write characters like you."

"You will. If you keep at it."

Lily took a breath. "I'm sorry about the Big Match."

"Ah. No sorry to me. To someone else. Perhaps?"

Lily nodded. "Yes, someone else."

"Your team is broken," Gung Gung said.

Broken like a smashed plate of wonton.

"Sad energy," Gung Gung said. "All around."

"I know. And I think I know how to fix it. I'd like to try."

"Oh? How?"

"Can we go to Asawa's?" Lily asked.

A few days later, Lily passed out aprons to each of her Leopard Sharks. She gave one to Coach too. The Asawa kitchen staff stood nearby, scratching their heads. They'd probably never seen an entire soccer team in their kitchen before.

"What's going on?" Deb asked her mom.

"Not sure," Coach said. "What's the flow, Lo? What's up?"

The team asked the same thing as they tied their aprons around their waists. Their chatter grew as noisy as a Big Match.

Lily banged a ladle against the stainless-steel worktable to get their attention. "Hey, Sharks," she said. "Thanks for coming. I know it's not our usual place."

"No kidding," Deb said, her arms crossed.

"How old is everyone here?" Anita asked.

"I bet they don't play soccer," Julie said.

"Maybe we can go to the park later," Toni said.

"Yeah, good idea," Deb said. "Lily can stay here if she wants."

Nerves shot up Lily's back. They were still annoyed with her, and she didn't blame them. Only Rosana remained quiet and waited for her to continue.

Something Gung Gung had said nudged her gently forward. *Sometimes bitter is good for you. Make you strong.*

She could do it.

"We're going to make wonton!" Lily said.

Her team suddenly grew quiet.

"It's a favorite dish here, and we're going to make it for them," Lily said. "It's a lot of work for one person to do." She glanced at Gung Gung. "All by himself."

When Gung Gung smiled back, Lily felt as if she might float among the fog, the sunshine, anything!

"Why don't we buy it?" Toni asked.

"Or eat at a restaurant?" Anita asked.

"We don't know how to make it," Rosana said.

"Yeah, how?" Deb said, uncrossing her arms.

"I'll show you. Come on! First, wash your hands," Lily said.

The Leopard Sharks gathered around the sink as water, hands, soap suds, and hand towels all moved in a whirl.

Next, Lily explained each ingredient laid out on the work-table. Of course, she told them how to do the shrimp. Then she began.

"Yat, yih, saam."

She placed the first finished wonton on a cookie sheet.

It glowed like sunlight peeking through the fog.

The team's faces lit up.

"Stellar!" Rosana said.

"Let me try," Anita said.

A chorus of *"Yat, yih, saam"* rang throughout the kitchen.

One, two, three.

Ich, ni, san.

Eyns, tsvey, dray.

A team of little hands danced around the wonton filling and skins. Skin rips and bulges appeared, but the Sharks kept at it, and didn't give up.

"Uno, dos, tres," Rosana sang. She held up her wonton like a trophy.

Soon, filling by filling, wrap by wrap, all the sad energy melted into giggles, laughter, and smiles.

Cookie sheets full of wonton lined the worktable, enough for a splendid feast. The kitchen staff scrambled to get more sheets. On the stove burners, water boiled in shiny stockpots, waiting to cook the homemade wonton.

Gung Gung chopped green onions for the soup. And while Bing started stir-frying vegetables in a wok, the flame sparkling, Lily got an idea.

"Can we make fried wonton, too?" Lily asked Gung Gung. "Didn't I like it as a baby? And so did my dad, right? Like in the picture in your room."

Gung Gung's eyebrows raised, and he stopped chopping. "*Haih ah.* Your father liked *jow* wonton very much."

Lily smiled. She had a feeling she'd like them, too.

Like on that day at Sampan, Lily sensed a memory passing before Gung Gung's eyes. A fond memory, sprinkled with a touch of sadness.

"Are you okay?" Lily asked, worried.

"Your great-grandmama fried wonton. Her favorite way to make it," he said. "Placed wonton in hot oil. Bubbles around the *pei.* Sizzled. Cooking oil smells. Stayed in her hair, skin, clothes for days. Good idea, Lily!"

Lily raised her arms, all wave-like.

"I love fried stuff, like french fries," Toni said.

"Or lumpia," Julie said.

"Taquitos!" Anita said.

The Leopard Sharks high-fived one another.

At the end of the counter, Deb and Coach were busy folding their wonton.

Lily gathered her courage as she walked toward them. "Those are really good." She pointed to Deb's wonton.

"Uh, thanks," Deb said.

"You must've made them before," Lily said.

"No, never," Deb said. "But I always wanted to."

"I was thinking. We could make them after a game sometime," Lily said. "My mom wants to make them more often."

Deb looked at her. "Really?"

"Sure," Lily said.

"I'm pretty hungry after games," Deb said.

"Me too," Lily said.

"Maybe we can make it for Miss Lu and our classmates," Deb said.

"Yeah, maybe," Lily said.

Deb and Coach both smiled.

When Lily turned to get more wonton skin, she noticed Gung Gung had been listening to their conversation. He leaned in and whispered, "Like your great-grandmama . . . you are the best wonton maker."

After all the wonton had been boiled or fried, the kitchen staff ladled the dumplings into steaming bowls of soup. The aroma made Lily's eyes water.

In the dining room, the seniors were ready. And hungry! Stomachs growled.

"Rosana," Lily said. "Surprise!"

Mr. and Mrs. Morales waved from a table with Rose, the needlepoint lady, and the mahjong players. Mr. Morales was pouring tea for everyone.

"I asked them to stay for wonton," Lily said.

Ro hugged Lily tight.

When each senior was given a bowl of soup, they nodded in gratitude. Huge smiles spread across everyone's faces. Soup steam fogged up one man's glasses.

When they started eating, they looked like they had found paradise.

"Ho ho sihk!" someone said. "Eat!"

"The finest!" Mr. Morales said.

"Such comfort!" Rose said.

"They're eating it! They like it! Hey, Lily!" The team gathered for one giant belly bump.

"I made that one," Rosana said, giggling.

"No, that's mine," Anita said.

"They like mine best," Toni said, laughing.

Ruth set a table especially for Lily's team. "Come on, ladies. You've earned this."

The Leopard Sharks and Coach sat down with their bowls of wonton before them. Together as one, like a well-trained soccer team, they blew on their soup and sipped with care.

The Sharks slurped, slurped, slurped!

The seniors slurped, slurped, slurped!

Before taking their seats, Gung Gung and Lily watched everyone eat.

"Beautiful," Gung Gung said.

"Ho leng," Lily said.

She slipped her arm around his waist, and he squeezed her shoulder. And held still for a moment longer.

THE END

GLOSSARY

of Cantonese (and Other Foreign) Words and Phrases

abuela y abuelo   Grandmother and grandfather in Spanish

ai-ya   An expression similar to "Oh no!" or "Oh my goodness!" The author grew up hearing this expression, used when a person expresses anger, surprise, or disbelief.

amorcito   Sweetie in Spanish

choh dai   "Sit down"

chow mein   A noodle dish mixed with meat and vegetables. The noodles are thin like spaghetti.

chow fun   A noodle dish similar to chow mein, but with thick rice noodles. Can be served wet with gravy or "dry-fried" (the author's favorite) without gravy.

dor dje   "Thank you" (used when receiving something, like a gift)

dim sum   Bite-sized Chinese dishes, such as ha gow, served in steamer baskets or small plates. In some restaurants, dim sum is served on little carts brought to your table.

Eyns, tsvey, dray "One, two, three" in Yiddish

foo jook   Dried bean curd

gei ho   "I am well," or "Not bad" (in answer to "How are you?")

gracias   "Thank you" in Spanish

gung gung   Maternal grandfather

ha gow   A shrimp dumpling

haih ah   An affirmative term that can mean "okay" or "yes"

ho   Good or well

ho leng   Beautiful

ho mh ho sihk mei ah?   "Tastes good?"

ho ho sihk   "Tastes good, yum!"

hau   Mouth

ich, ni, san   "One, two, three" in Japanese

jo san   "Good morning"

joong   Shaped like pyramids, these tamale-like Chinese bundles consist of sticky rice, meat, egg, nuts, beans, and other ingredients steamed and wrapped together in bamboo leaves, then tied with string.

jow   Fried

lumpia   A fried spring roll from the Philippines and Indonesia

maan maan   "Slow down"

mahjong   A game similar to the card game gin rummy, except it is played with tiles

mein   Noodles

mh goi   "Thank you" (used when receiving help or a service)

neih ho ma?   "How are you?" Or "Are you well?"

neih le?	"And you?"
queso	Cheese
pei	Skin, like the skin of a wonton or a piece of fruit, like an apple
siet	Stone
sui mai	A pork or beef round-shaped dumpling, served while eating dim sum
taquito	A fried or baked rolled taco with filling
tien	Rice field
uno, dos, tres	"One, two, three" in Spanish
yat, yih, saam	"One, two, three" in Cantonese

ABOUT THE AUTHOR

Frances Lee Hall (1964–2016)

Frances was born and raised in San Francisco and graduated from San Francisco State University. She worked in television production as a writer and a producer for KQED, KRON, and Tech TV, as well as independently. She won three Emmys from the Academy of Television Arts and Sciences. She attended Vermont College of Fine Arts, graduating in 2008 with an MFA in Writing for Children and Young Adults. She taught and edited writers of all ages and lived in Pacifica, California, with her husband and daughter. Homemade wonton was one of her favorite dishes.

GRAND PATRONS

Ann Jacobus Kordahl
Annemarie O'Brien
Agatha & Aaron Veng
Barbara Younger
Bonnie Lee
Cathren Page
Christine Dowd
Cynthia Leitich Smith
Dian Curtis Regan
Evan Lai
Evelyn, Lance, & Emmie Hall
Helen Kemp Zax
Javier Valencia
Katherine Applegate
Katherine Huey
Kay Mansfield

Kelly Bennett
Lyn Miller-Lachmann
Maria Kawah
Marietta B. Zacker
Martha Graham
Mary Atkinson
Mary Ginnane
May Key C. Lee
Melissa Christy Buron
Mima Tipper
Nancy Bo Flood
Nancy Juliber
Nancy Thalia Reynolds
Nora Ericson
Paul G. & Colleen Lee
Rita Williams-Garcia
Sharon Stettin

INKSHARES

INKSHARES is a reader-driven publisher and producer based in Oakland, California. Our books are selected not by a group of editors, but by readers worldwide.

While we've published books by established writers like *Big Fish* author Daniel Wallace and *Star Wars: Rogue One* scribe Gary Whitta, our aim remains surfacing and developing the new author voices of tomorrow.

Previously unknown Inkshares authors have received starred reviews and been featured in the *New York Times*. Their books are on the front tables of Barnes & Noble and hundreds of independents nationwide, and many have been licensed by publishers in other major markets. They are also being adapted by Oscar-winning screenwriters at the biggest studios and networks.

Interested in making your own story a reality? Visit Inkshares.com to start your own project or find other great books.

CPSIA information can be obtained
at www.ICGtesting.com
Printed in the USA
BVHW080800161218
535725BV00002B/209/P